# It Can
# Happen
# In A Minute

## S.M. JOHNSON

Copyright 2006 by S.M. Johnson
ISBN: 0975945343

Edited by Anthony Whyte
Design/Photogaphy: Jason Claiborne

First printing Augustus Publishing paperback November 2006

AUGUSTUS
PUBLISHING

**AugustusPublishing.com**
33 Indian Road New York, New York 10034

# Acknowledgments

Thanks to Kimberly Brooks, Mary Cole, Tenika Daye, Monica Hayes, Marina Kenney, Sabrina Kenney, Brenda Tyger, and Jacqueline Shuler. Good-looking Jerome Brooks and James Ruffin for reading the first couple of pages and giving me support.


# Special Dedication

William Watkins, thank you for giving me a B when I read the first couple of pages while you were on lock down.
One Love!


*Good-looking out to the Augustus Management Team. Jason Claiborne, Joy Leftow and Tamiko Maldonado. Special thanks to Lydia Hyatt.*


*Go hard or go home.*

Haters don't want me to grow.

Always trying to block my flow

stopping my success.

If I let them, that sure be a mess.

A seed that flowers,

I'll mature for all to witness my show.

Lord guide my soul as I leap to the

other side of the rainbow.

**smjohnson**

# Prologue

I got on the elevator and was surprised when someone wearing a ski mask jumped out of nowhere. He started pulling at me and I grabbed the laundry door. He was strong and pulled me so hard that eventually I had to let go.

He pushed me in a darkened room. This bastard could see my swollen stomach but started pushing me against the window. I was facing a window with an opaque glass. I tried to turn around resisting but to no avail. He brutally yanked my shorts down. I heard his zipper and glanced over my shoulder. I saw an old mattress on the floor. I was hoping that this bitch-ass nigga wasn't gonna ask me to the fuck lay down.

I had to think and fast. I felt his hands all over my body and his penis hard against my butt. I put two gold rings in my mouth and started shaking. He was trying to penetrate and I was screaming. My heart was pounding in my chest when I heard footsteps.

# 1

I remember sitting by the speakers at my babysitters' house, singing along with Bobby Womack's: If loving you is wrong I don't wanna be right. Back in the days I was grooving, listening to all the good music, growing up in Miami. Man that was a lot of fun.

Everyday there was sunshine. My friends and I played childhood games like boys-chase-girls, which would quickly transform to hide-and-go-get. I was the first to jump at any opportunity to play. A fast runner, I would be the first inside the house. Once Tony Ward moved to the neighborhood, I didn't mind getting caught. Both he and his brother Darnell were fine.

Tony was dark-skinned and Darnell was brown skinned. In the seventies, dark-skinned brothers weren't the thing, but I was down from the moment boys started checking me out. I was eleven and didn't want to be the only one feeling on myself.

My name is Samone, and early in my life looking out for number one became my song. I have a little sister, Shellie. She was my mother's pet. Her spoiled ass told everything, so I had to keep her out of my business.  Because if my mother, Mamacita, found out that I was flirting with boys, it would be over for my cute ass.  I had a better shape than most girls older than me, even my girlfriends hated on me.

"Girl, get your big butt out of the way," my friends would always tease.  I knew they were just hating.  My girlfriends may have been jealous over my figure but the boys appreciated it.  None of my girlfriends had curves.

Kathy was skinny, and Gumdrop was iron board straight.  Tangy was a tomboy and once threatened to beat up Tony.  Tangy had a huge family and if Tony didn't go with her, she would have put one of her big, black, greasy-assed cousins on him.  Tony was cruisin me at the time.

It was early summer and we were all hanging at the pool when he told me what was actually going on.  He suggested that we act like we weren't together anymore.  I thought about it.

"Okay," I said and walked away disappointed.

I really didn't like the idea but would have done anything for his chocolate-ness.  I was going to miss his curly hair and those pretty white teeth.

Later that same day Kathy acted as if she wanted to bring me the same news.

"Don't you know that Tony seeing Tangy…"

"He already told me."  I said abruptly cutting her off.  I wasn't in the mood for her nosey ass chit-chat.

School was out and this summer was going to be different.  I wasn't making the annual trip to Orlando.  I was spending the summer with my father.  He lived in D.C., where I was born nearly twelve years ago. My mother was young and couldn't take care of a newborn. When I was three months old, she sent me to live with my grandmother. I wound up living away from my father. I had waited a long time for this minute.

Finally, I was at the airport on my way back to visit my father.

"Be good and don't act up and give your daddy any problems, girl. Behave yourself like your sister Shellie would."

"Flight 2-0-2 to D.C. now boarding at gate seven..."

I rolled my eyes at Shellie before walking to the airplane. She must have told Mamacita something about me again. Maybe she saw me kissing Tony goodbye. It didn't faze me none. I was on my way out.

I stared at the clouds from my window seat on the plane and the excitement surged through me as the plane soared. The seatbelts restrictions were lifted and my thoughts quickly changed to my father. He was a busy man. I knew he worked a lot. He had been to Florida to see me on different occasions. The first time he visited was when I had been hit by a car. I was in the first grade, and he came to visit me in the hospital. The other time was on my eighth birthday. He took me to Disney World. Another time, he took me to get my ears pierced. That particular time, he and my mother spent all night in her bedroom. The squeaking of their bed kept me up most of the night.

My mother always told me that my father and I were alike, though she did not say how. I quickly lost all thoughts as I gazed at the clouds. I closed my eyes wishing that I would have a great time.

The buildings became visible as the plane started to descend. I could see the bright lights of the city. Suddenly the impact of the moment hit me; this summer was going to be different from all the other summers, for real! Other summers had been spent with Grandma Smith in Orlando. This time I didn't want to know anyone but my father.

I was waiting in the lounge when a tall dark and ruggedly handsome man walked toward me. I immediately knew who he was.

"Samone, it's so good to see you. How was the flight?" He asked.

"It was really cool..." I let my voice trail because I was unsure exactly how to address him.

"Are you hungry?"

I heard the question but was still caught up in my thoughts. I nodded.

"I made us some fried chicken," he said leading me to his car. As we drove on the highway in his blue Caddy, I sat quietly staring out the window. It was my way to prevent myself from staring. Mamacita always told me that it was impolite to stare. He made a turn close to what looked like a zoo. I couldn't resist.

"Is that a zoo?" I asked excitedly.

"Yes, my place is close by," he said.

A minute later my father made the announcement.

"Here we are," he said.

"You live really close to the zoo." I noted.

"Yeah, walking distance, Samone, there'll be time for that."

He guided me to a big building and we got on the elevator. I blinked rapidly, surprised that we had arrived at a nice, well furnished, one-bedroom apartment. Best of all he lived around the corner from the zoo. I couldn't imagine being so close to the zoo. In Florida the zoo was far away from my home.

We went inside and immediately after washing my hands father gave me a plate. I ate at the dining room table while father sat in the living room watching baseball on the television. The chicken was greasy but I was hungry. I was still thinking about what to call him when he walked into the kitchen.

"Are you finished, my baby-girl?" he asked.

"Yes, daddy," I answered faintly.

He showed me where I would be sleeping and went back to watching the game. It had been a long day and I was tired. That night I slept peacefully in my father's bed. In the morning I awoke and smelled just like a man. I wandered through the apartment looking for him.

"Daddy, daddy, are you here?"

No answer. He was gone but had left me a note. My uncle would be coming around to see me later.

I showered and watched television while I waited. Later, I heard the doorbell.

"Who is it?" I asked.

"Samone, this your Uncle Black." He announced. I buzzed him in and when he came up I was happy to see him but still dealing with the disappointment of not seeing my father off.

"Hi, Uncle Black," I greeted him with a smile.

"Hey girl, you're growing up. I bet you haven't seen your

grandmother in Portsmouth, VA?" he asked. "Do you want to go visit?"

"Sure," I said staring at him. He removed his sunglasses and it was clear that he looked like my father, only shorter.

"Oh by the way, this is my friend, Carmen."

"Hi Carmen," I smiled. Despite her make-up, she seemed really young. She must have been older because she was already drinking dark liquor.

"Everyone set, alright let's go," Uncle Black said.

I sat in the back seat and listened as old soft jams played on. My uncle and his girlfriend were sipping and singing away. The car dashed along the highway.

"Tidewater eighty five miles," she yelled excitedly.

I closed my eyes until we arrived in Norfolk. We stopped briefly and I saw a shipyard for the first time in my life. My uncle spoke to some men on the dock then we were off to Portsmouth.

"Ida Barbour." Uncle Black announced. "This is where your grandmother lives."

I glanced at the low cost houses. There were a lot of people living close together.

"Grandma lives in the projects," he said pointing. I smiled.

I had been to the projects before. My cousins lived in Liberty City. I found that there was always something to do there. People were always outside.

It was about ten o'clock on a Sunday; my grandmother wasn't home from church yet. I didn't know a soul but was ready to go outside. I saw some older boys rolling dice by the trash can, and some girls my age just hanging out. My Uncle put my bags upstairs and introduced me to my Aunt Dottiea. We chit chatted for a minute then we walked outside.

Later that evening, I sat on the porch being nosy. Dusk came too quickly and I couldn't wait for the next day to come, so that I could really see what was going on.

"You have a lot of cousins, some living across the railroad tracks in Swanson Homes—your Aunt Lane, your cousin Carlethia, and Marvin." My Aunt Dottiea said joining me on the porch.

She stopped and stared then pointed.

"Right up them steps, on the corner, that's your older cousin, May. She just had a newborn son, Lil' Jake."

"Can I go say hi to them?"

"Sure, go on, girl. You need not even introduce yourself, one look atcha and they'll know whose child you are." She smiled.

I walked over and visited with my other family.

"Come inside for a few," my cousin offered.

We were barely a few minutes inside the house when there was knocking on the door. A short dark-skinned woman walked in and came up the steps.

"Hello," she said giving me a hug. I returned her hug but had no idea who she was.

"That's your Grandmother, Samone," May said.

"My grandmother, wow. Now I know where dad gets all his good looks from."

"Your grandfather was good looking too." She smiled showing a beautiful set of teeth.

"Samone just came…"

"Are you hungry?" my grandmother asked with her arm around me.

"Yes, grandma," I said feeling her warmth.

"Good, cause we got some kale greens, roast, rice, and lots of ice tea." She guided me down the stairs.

I knew about collards, but not kale. I loved all kinds of greens and she was my grandmother, so I knew the food had to be good.

"Hmm, grandma that sounds yummy." I said walking back to the house with her. I ate heartily and then it was lights-out for me.

# 2

In the morning after taking a bath, I watched television. My cousin, May came by and introduced me to her younger brother, Stephon and sister, Melva. They took me to the center where dances were held. After that we went hanging in the Swanson Homes and then we went to Douglas Park. My cousins were fun and we were out to the wee hours of the morning.

May made sure it was okay with Aunt Mattie to let me stay with her. I had big fun during the time I spent with my cousins but I was ready to see my father. He was driving down at the end of the week.

The weekend was here in a flash and there was a fish-fry over Aunt Mattie's house. I had no idea that they would fry fish outside on the grill. Outside baby! I tell you it was the bomb. The fish and cornbread ruled. We all ate and chatted up a storm.

After the party, my father and I began the trek back to his home in the District of Columbia. He looked sharp with a goatee wearing a white linen suit. I felt safe with him. It was like when daddy's around, Samone don't want nothing else.

"Daddy, grandma is really cool and she's very pretty." I said putting away the fried fish and cornbread grandma packed for me.

"Yeah, hmm you think so, huh?"

"Huh, uh, now I know where we got our good looks from." I smiled and daddy chuckled.

The trip was long and I was feeling delighted to be riding with him. I tried my best to stay awake but eventually fell asleep as he drove.

"Samone, Samone, we're home," he said gently shaking me.

"Okay, daddy," I yawned struggling to a slow rouse. By the time I walked inside the apartment, I was fully awake. We had company. There were people everywhere. I went to the bedroom and saw people drinking and sticking their hands in a crystal bowl, sprinkling bud on paper.

I waved at Uncle Black and Carmen. She was always smiling. They raised their glasses and I smiled back. Daddy escorted me to the bedroom and made sure everyone was out before he left me alone.

"Are you okay?"

I nodded.

"If you want anything, just call me. I'll be outside watching the playoffs."

I sat in his chair listening to song after song being played, wishing that my cousins had made the drive back with us.

Glancing around the room, I saw jackets and sweaters. Then I noticed the opened bottle of liquor. My curiosity got the best of me. I eased out of the chair and swallowed some of it. It was strong and made me cough. Ever so carefully I drank some more. Light-headedness overcame me and I sat back in daddy's easy chair. Thoughts did laps in my head. I felt like I was drowning, swimming round and round. Everything became fuzzy. Eventually I was able to close my eyes and fell sound asleep.

# 3

The following morning I awoke and knew something had happened. I was still wearing the same top but I was completely naked below the waist. When I tried to move a pain shot through my entire body. I gingerly made my way to the bathroom. Each step made the pain even worse. I was in agony by the time I closed the door. I turned the light switch on and saw tears in my eyes. Something was terribly wrong. My legs had blood stains on them and there was this dried, white stuff all over my face. I felt faint and sat on the toilet. I saw a creamy stuff coming from inside me.

Sitting awhile allowed the wooziness time wear off. I jumped in the shower and scrubbed my body. The shower not only helped cleanse me but the pain slowly went away. I got dressed and on my way back to the room I heard daddy snoring and saw a woman's naked behind over his waist. I angrily stomped around the room. They never untwined or even took notice of me and kept snoring loudly.

The kitchen was dirty and filled with empty glasses and bottles. There were dishes and half eaten chicken piled in corners. The place looked nothing like when I first came. I wanted to clean up. I didn't know where to start so I poured a glass of water and went back to the bedroom. The pain in my private area was going away. I fell asleep.

Later, Daddy woke me. I never mentioned what happened. There was some amount of embarrassment and I didn't know where to start. How do I begin? Instead I feigned a smile when he offered to take me shopping and dinner. I walked outside and noticed that daddy had done a good job of tidying up.

We walked to the car and I remained very quiet but my mind was busy. I wondered what happened and who had done it? I tried but couldn't remember anything. At the mall I watched him greeting his many friends.

"Breezy," they would holler.

He was well known, because wherever we went people knew his name. I finally asked daddy.

"Why do they call you Breezy daddy?"

"Breezy? Cause that's how I am. It's my nickname." He smiled as we took our seats in the restaurant. I wanted to tell daddy about what happened when I awoke this morning. I changed my mind because I didn't want him to be angry at me and tell Mamacita. I knew for sure she would blame everything on me. I could hear the annoying questions: Why did you drink the liquor, Samone? Instead I thought of the fun I had shopping with my daddy.

Over the next couple of days everything got dreary and boring. My father left me alone at home, he had to work. Then he hung with his friends. I watched television until I was bored. One day I decided to go walking down the hall. I met Janet but she didn't mind staying inside, she told me it was due to her illness.

She was afraid to go outside. All she wanted to do was stay in the house and eat all day. I mean she was really afraid of going outside. She didn't even want to attend school. I told her about what happened but acted as if it wasn't me. She was smart enough to talk with.

"This girl woke up and found all her clothes off?" Her question came with haste and great curiosity.

"Well, it wasn't all her clothes, just her jeans and panties. She was covered on top." I explained.

"I don't know, I mean this girl had skeet all over her face and secretions coming from her private area."

"Yeah, I think so…"

"Well something must have happened. Someone might've put some type of drug in the drink and you know…take advantage of her…my mother is a nurse and could tell you more. Do you wanna ask her?"

"No, that's alright. It was only a movie…"

"What movie was that?"

"I don't even remember the name of it. It's really not that urgent." I thought for a moment then wondered aloud. "The fourth of July is almost here. What are you doing?" I asked changing the subject.

"The same ol', barbecue, eat and then I'll turn down the chance to go to the park and watch fireworks."

"Wow, that sounds exciting," I said.

"It's exciting if you're into that. But remember, I can't stand the crowd or being outside." She deadpanned.

She was depressing me. I left her with my mind clinging to the thought of spending a wonderful Independence Day with daddy and watching fireworks in the Nation's Capital.

Maybe it was because I got caught up with the idea of spending independence Day with my dad here in DC. Whatever it was managed to push the idea of telling my dad about what happened in the back of my mind. The excitement of seeing all the fireworks was too thrilling for me to mess up.

The holiday came fast and daddy gave me the treat of my life. We went to Malcolm-X Park. There were live bands and lots of fireworks. The park was crowded with people and police were all around. Later, we stopped at Uncle Black's for barbecue and the food was fantastic. All of daddy's friends were hanging out and having a good time. Things went really smooth. I did not drink any liquor and I had a lot of fun.

I didn't want to cause any further problems and decided to forget about what happened in daddy's room. I cheered and enjoyed an amazing fireworks show. I had a great time.

I slept most of the next day.

Before I knew it, Wednesday night came. Daddy informed me that reservations had been made for me to stay a week in Orlando Florida.

"Your Grandma Smith wants to see you before you go

back to school," he said.

It was all set. I was to visit with my grandmother— Mamacita's mother. I was leaving Saturday morning.

"Dag!" I said to myself.

"You're always welcome back honey. We'll see each other again."

Just when I thought that I was about to get to know my daddy and maybe have fun, I've got to leave.

The weekend quickly came and sadly I was packed and ready to go. I hugged and kissed daddy goodbye at the airport. With some sense of relief, I walked away from my father and waved until I couldn't see him anymore.

On the plane I closed my eyes and thought about my vacation. Despite everything it had been a great summer. First, it was the Capital, and now I was heading to Orlando.

I could go swimming, play kick ball and hide-go-seek. Then I could visit my cousins, aunts, uncles, and grandmother. I'll see all my friends who live in Comstock. It was a big neighborhood and everyone owned their own home.

Uncle Buddy and Auntie had property and so did Grandma. There were avocado trees, peaches in the back of Uncle Buddies' house. Also he had rows of orange pecan and grapefruit trees.

My vacation was turned out to be wonderful. I couldn't wait to write about my trip on the first day of school. The teachers always asked and boy will I have a lot to talk about.

They were there waiting for me at the airport and I was tired as ever. I was happy to see them but fell asleep in the backseat.

I think I slept the entire time I was there. Grandma kept asking me if I felt okay. Even though I kept telling her I was alright, she kept giving me extra food. She thought it was because I missed my daddy.

Needless to say, I did nothing for the whole week. Then on Saturday I went swimming with my uncle and grandmother. We headed back to grandma's home after I started vomiting. My uncle thought it was motion sickness. My grandmother gave me a stern look when she asked.

"Girl, what's really the matter with you. You couldn't be…" her voice trailed, but her brows were knitted in suspicion.

The conversation was cut short by my uncle's erratic driving.

"Boy, look where the hell you're going!" My grandmother screamed.

We eventually reached home and over the next few days, grandma gave me all sorts of home grown remedies. The medication served to push all the bad thoughts from my mind.

On my way to the airport grandma was still fussing about my uncle's driving. She felt that he would make me sick and vomit again. I didn't. We arrived I was checked in and found my seat. I fell asleep contemplating what was wrong with me.

Not long after that I felt someone gently shaking me. I awoke and heard a voice.

"Did you have a good time?" the flight attendant asked.

"Yes, I did." I yawned nodding.

"We're in Miami and you can identify who will be here to

get you then..."

"Mamacita, my mother, she's coming to pick me up."

"Okay, then lets get your luggage and we'll go see her."

"Okay," I said.

Once the flight attendant made sure that I had identified my party to pick me up, I was off with Mamacita. It was late evening and there was dimness over the whole place. I missed the fireworks in D.C.

"You had a lot of fun, huh?"

"Yes, and daddy bought me some new clothes."

"Good, I don't have to buy you any."

My mother always had a way of squashing the fun. It was back to the basics.

"A lot of your friends came around asking if you were back," Mamacita said as we made our way home.

Finally I was there. I was happy that my friends missed me. One thing I knew Mamacita and Daddy had in common was that they believe in waking up early in the morning to take care of business. I couldn't wait to go outside to see who called themselves going with my boyfriend. I was tired and avoided my nosy sister Shellie as I quickly went to sleep.

The next morning after Mamacita left, I was out and about. I saw Tangy, the bully.

"Hi ya doin', Samone?" She asked greeting me.

"I'm fine, Tangy. How're you?" Why are trying to be nice? I wanted to ask as she approached me.

"Samone, you know Reds and Tony messin' with each other. They go together for real. They've been huggin' and kissin'

at the movies on 183rd Street." Tangy said sounding disappointed. I guess that was really what she wanted to tell me. I knew
Tony's new girl, Redds.

"Oh really, her grandmother is letting her outside?" I
asked wanting to laugh aloud. Inside I was cracking up. Tangy
knew that I used to mess with Tony. Wait until I see him, I
thought.

"Gumdrop is back. She went to Deland."

"Oh really...?" I asked.

"Yup," Tangy said. "She went away for the summer, and
skinny ass Kathy went to Tallahassee." She continued. She was
shifting in place the way boxers do before a fight. I had to get
away from her.

"Where did you go, Tangy?" I asked.

"I...ah...I was supposed to go somewhere but something
came up and I wind up not going anywhere."

"I had mucho fun in D.C., and Va., and what can I say
about Orlando? Well, got to go, girl." I bragged.

I walked away from Tangy wearing a proud smile. Now I
was rushing to find my girls Kathy and Gumdrop and let them
know what was going down. I knew exactly where they would be.

"Oh, I already knew all that..." Kathy said cutting me off.

"How you know all that?" I asked.

"Who else, but from Tangy, herself," Kathy answered.

"What you gonna do?" Gumdrop asked.

"You know Tony and his brother are going to the movies
Sunday, right?" I asked.

"Yeah and..." Kathy rejoined.

"Well..." I started.

"Samone, you gotta ask my mama if I could go to the movies." Gumdrops interrupted. "You know if you ask, she would let me go."

"All right," I said staring at her.

That was only part of the set-up. We would continue to scheme.

"And let's get there real early so we can wait for him."

Our plan involved luring Redds outside. There was a glitch when we found that the only way Redds was able to come outside was when she took out the trash. We waited for the chance. Kathy's report during that week was always the same.

"Redds came outside today with the trashcan. She was out for there for awhile. Tangy was talking to her then Miss Rose comes running for her."

"I'm going to knock on the door!" I said getting fed-up with waiting.

"They are in Gools, Samone." Kathy said.

"Gools, ooh way down South Miami, where all the fine boys live." Gumdrop chimed.

We were in the complex talking when a bunch of older teenage boys pulled up and got out a car. Tony exited the front seat and about four cute boys got out the back. One was Tony's brother, Darnell.

As soon as I saw Tony I just wanted to kiss his beautiful lips. All I wanted to do was just to feel his tongue and knowing he was with Redds all I felt was pain.

I was caught up in my misery when suddenly I heard

someone shouting.

"Samone, you home."

I turned and saw Tony's brother, Darnell waving but I was focused on Tony. He acted like he didn't see me and kept his eyes glued on his mother who was waiting to greet them.

"Hi Samone, how was your trip? Where did you go?" She asked in one sentence.

"I was in Washington DC, then I went to Norfolk, VA, and also spent a week in Orlando." I answered.

I began to wonder if I should bother to mention Portsmouth, Va., or my daddy and godmother taking me shopping, or my trip to Orlando.

"Sounds to me like you had a great summer?" Tony's mother said.

"Yes Ms Ward!" I almost screamed.

"You have such a pretty smile, Samone." She was always leaving with a compliment and making me smile.

"What's up pretty?" Tony greeted as he walked over.

"Samone's smile," his mother said walking away.

"Oh, yeah, and her pretty brown eyes," Tony said. His smile made me melt.

"Redds want you Tony," Darnell said butting in.

Darnell and I have been pretty cool since I can remember, but he acts like a little faggot. He, Tony and I were all born in March. Tony and I act so mature but not Darnell. I was still caught up in Tony's stare, when I heard him calling my name.

"Samone..."

"Huh?" I answered giving him my best dreamy eyes.

"Samone you've been away, out of town, huh? Are you going to the movies Sunday?"

"Yeah and why are you asking?"

"I'm going, that's why."

"Me and my cousins are going. Don't be tellin' everybody, all right?"

"Whatever..."

"I'm about to play some softball." Tony turned to walk away.

"I'm playin' too." I said whirling and following right behind his fine ass.

Tangy was trying to coax Miss Rose to let Redds come outside to play. Tangy who had told me about Redds, now wanted to be on Redds' side. That sneaky bald-headed, tomboy bitch was trying to start something. I wasn't about to fight over no boy, but if someone hit me, it would be on.

Tony and his cousin, Rob were the team captains. All that was needed were two more players and both teams would be even. Redds and Tangy came and Tony let his cousin pick Redds. I was on the team with Tangy. If any of us screwed up a play, she would try and show off, by getting in our faces and fussing trying to scare us. She was a fake who thought she was all that.

I could hit, run, and catch with the best of the boys. Kathy could hit and run, but wasn't good in fielding, she couldn't catch. Gumdrop could hit, but had no speed. She was easily distracted and couldn't catch her own breath. As the game progressed our team was down and losing. It was our turn to field.

Tangy tried to change the course of the game by making

a ridiculous demand.

"Let's play hide-go-get," she shouted.

"How you gonna wanna stop like that, Tangy?" Rob asked.

"Cause I can," Tangy answered.

"You baldheaded-ass we won't play no hide-go-get. Who the fuck gon' chase you?" Rob asked.

I started laughing, and then everybody else did.

"If you act like a nigga, I'm going to treat you like one. You better stay in a girl's, place."

Tangy kept her mouth shut.

"Okay, we'll play. Count to ten first." Gumdrop said knowing she can't run. Her hot-butt was always trying to get caught. Who was Tony going to catch? I wondered.

"Redds, you come inside." Miss Rose yelled out the window.

I think she hated to be in the house by herself. Redds was clearly mad.

"Ma, can I stay out?"

"Come inside now."

She left and the chase was on. Tangy sat on the steps looking disappointed. Darnell urged her to participate, but her feelings were hurt and she player-hated while Tony chased me. I ran all the way down to the rental office, dipped upstairs to the meter-room and let him catch up. There we made out wildly. He kissed and rubbed his hands all over my bootie, my tits. He mde me moist. Sweat poured from our hot bodies. We were there for a long time. Tony was working hard to get some of that you-know-what.

"Redds can hardly come outside." He said later as we walked back. We promised to meet Sunday at the movies.

I was in dreamland that Sunday when Tony sat with me for a little while. It didn't really matter that he left to hang with his cousins. I didn't even remember what the movie was about.

Monday morning was the first day of school. Redds knocked on Tony's door and they walked to school together. When Kathy, Gumdrop and I got to school, we heard all about it. Darnell and I were in the same fifth grade class and he told me everything. That was the good thing, the bad thing, Darnell was still  a silly-ass boy.

One day while the class was still in session, Darnell was rocking back and forth while lying on the floor. He was pretending to pass out or something. It was near the end of the school day. I needed to turn my assignment in. As I walked pass Darnell, he opened his eyes and smiled. After class, Darnell came over to where I was.

"I saw your panties," he said with a smirk on his face.

"You did not," I said.

"They were white," he said confirming the color.

"You're such a kid."

"At least you weren't cuttin' cheese like the other girls." He and his friends laughed.

I was mad and all I could think about was to wear shorts. I told Mamacita I need to wear shorts under my dress. Boy, can I tell you about growing pains.

# 4 | CATCHING HELL

I was getting fatter and fatter. I ate a lot and always had an appetite. Tony and I made out a lot and each time we did, he wanted to go further and further. One evening when Mamacita and Shellie had left for a parent meeting at her school, I let him in and he tried to stick his little head inside me. It didn't go all the way in. We came close to doing it and that was the first time Tony told me he loved me.

Mamacita was always a trip, but became even worse. Somehow the word got around about Tony and me and then things changed. All the boys began to notice me. I mean really notice me, like Kent, the sexiest guy in school stepped up. He was a chocolate boy, with bow-legs. Oh my, yeah! I was really hot. Every time he was around, I got a tingling sensation from my head to my toes.

One day I was hanging out with my girls, looking at boys. Mamacita rolled up on me with her friend, Paula.

"You better keep your head in those books and stop looking at those little piss tail boys." She yelled embarrassing me. Then she grabbed me and took me home.

Everyone made fun of the incident. I became the laughing stock.

Mamacita must have been going loca. Kathy's mother had no problems; none at all. In fact Kathy could go to the movies with the boy she was dating, a boy named Arthur. He lived in a nice house over in Carol City. Once Kathy and I went over to Arthur's house and his mother gave Kathy great respect. I'm talking mad love. She was happy to see her. The family greeted her warmly. She was twelve. Kathy could breathe. Unlike Mamacita, her mother never smothered her.

Two months into the school term I was so fat that my once tiny boobs were now popping out of everything I wore. I was still making out with Tony and everyone wanted to talk to me. I mean everywhere I went people stared.

Then just as suddenly as it started, my popularity ended. First, I saw less and less of Tony. He wouldn't come around anymore and when I tried to see Kent, he ignored me. It turned out that nobody in school wanted to talk to me. It was as if I had developed the plague or something.

I began worrying about it and one day I passed out at school. Waking up groggy in the emergency room of the hospital, I saw Mamacita crying. She walked over to me.

"It was that piss-tail, Tony wasn't it?" Mamacita asked,

tears in her eyes.

I was held overnight for observation. Due to the risk of death to the mother and child, the pregnancy was terminated. It felt like they were tearing my insides out, bit by bit. Thank God, the pain was short. The doctors didn't prescribe painkillers but I took them anyway. Sleep still didn't come too easy. I tried putting everything from my mind but it just wouldn't go away. The eventual exhaustion occurred.

Mamacita kept me out of school for the next two weeks. She was embarrassed over the incident.

"Now you know what I'm talkin' bout!"

It became her mantra for the evil that boys do to unsuspecting girls.

After a while, Kathy went to Tallahassee, saying she will be back in fourteen days. Weeks turned into months. She was registered for some of my seventh grade classes, but she never showed. My friend had moved away.

Gumdrop stopped by every now and then. I would see her at the mall, but her visits came less frequent. I could hardly go out and when I did, Shellie had to tag along. Life certainly was no fun.

# 5

For my thirteenth birthday Mamacita, to my surprise, threw me a party. She made sure only my girlfriends and family were there along with plenty of hotdogs, potato chips, punch, ice-cream, and cake. There was music, some presents, cards with money. All the girls laughed and danced, it was a great time.

Grandma Smith came from Orlando along with my cousins. She pulled me to the side and spoke to me in a serious tone.

"You're growing into a real woman real fast. Now, Samone you've got to be very careful cause it only take a minute and shit will happen." She said batting her eyes wildly and giving me a brown envelope. I smiled when I saw that it was from daddy and had my name on it. Ms. Samone Malinda Johnson, 3949 183rd St., NW Miami, FL. 33055, it read. A big smile crossed my lips when i opened it and saw the money order in a card from her and daddy.

"Thank you grandma," I said hugging her.

"Promise you're going to be careful. And please stop messing with these boys," she said. She pulled me real close and continued speaking. "Samone, last summer when you kept getting sick and had to sleep all the time, you could've been pregnant then right?"

"Grandma I don't think I was. Tony and I..." My voice trailed and I couldn't look in her eyes.

"Why you all off to the side? Come out and party with the rest of us."

It was Mamacita. The look on her face told me she knew that something serious was being discussed. Luckily, she wanted to lighten the mood. I went out and enjoyed the party with my friends.

I was older so Mamacita let me have my own phone. Shellie began acting like she had so much to talk about. She always wanted to use up my minutes. One day, Shellie broke down.

"Don't nobody call me?" She yelled in the midst of throwing her fit.

Mamacita let her have it. Then cut her eyes at me. Seemed like, for once, she was on my side. I closed my door wearing a grin.

New people were constantly moving to the neighborhood. A family moved into the townhouse where Tangy and her family had lived. The entire neighborhood had been glad when they moved.

Tangy's cousin was all right. I missed how he whistled at me whenever I walked by. Plus he was a real good softball player.

I went back to school. Everything was still junior high— older boys, new jeans Sassoon, Jordache, Sergio's. The fashion was changing and Mamacita was still complaining about the prices. She never changed. She still treated me bad. I had no new jeans, but she bought herself couple of her favorite polyester action slacks. Mamacita made me sick.

She'd get old clothes from her co-workers, and after wearing it, she'd try to pass it on to me. Damn, she was setting me up to be a failure. My classmates laughed at me. I was wearing bell-bottoms jeans, long after they were played. I needed help.

Sitting outside one day, feeling depressed, I saw a motorcycle flying down the street it was Uncle Raymond. I took off running immediately. Shellie was right behind me. We beat him home, shoved things under the bed and made it orderly. If our room wasn't clean there would be no money.

I was out of breath getting things back in order. We were a little worried when he said nothing. When Mamacita came home, he took her grocery shopping and gave us fifty dollars each. Thank God for Uncle Raymond. Shellie and I went to the Flea Market. I bought a pair of Jordache and a nice shirt to match. Shellie purchased her some Sassoons and a top. Mamacita was happy when she saw our outfits.

"You both look really good," she said and gave us fifty more dollars. We went back to the Flea Market. Shellie bought a shirt, just like mine, but in a different color, v-neck in the front and back—you couldn't tell us nothing.

When we got back Uncle Raymond was drinking brew.

"Now it's skating rink time. Roller skate time, baby, let's go." He shouted, rearing to bounce. Uncle Raymond was about having fun. He was a very good skater, dancing away on his skates when a skate guard knocked him down. The next thing I saw was Uncle Raymond zooming past and knocking the guard down. We were tossed out and wound up at another rink. Hanging with Uncle Raymond was a lot of fun.

Mamacita allowed me out a little bit more and I started going to high school dances. Space Funk DJ's was my favorite. When they were at Miami Garden's skating rink, I had to be there. Shellie was right with me. Night time enjoying the nightlife was where it was at. She was eleven and I was thirteen and we hung out in the skating rink.

I went skating all the time. Then they added another room just so people could dance. That's where I was doing my thing. Space Funk always jammed all the b-bop songs.

On any given night of the weekend I was saying: Oh, damn, look at all those Liberty City niggas. I know I got to get at least two good numbers. The joints used to be packed. One night I saw Meme from school. She was always hanging out.

"What's up Samone?"

"What's up Meme?"

"Samone, girl, you see all those city niggas in here? You know they stand out. They are so damn fine and their pockets are phat."

"Amen to that," I said snapping my fingers.

"Samone, here comes two fine ones heading our way," Meme said.

They approached us, stood in our space and started dancing. They sweated us as we were bumping and grinding all night long. They were flashing money. We got their numbers. That was cool. They asked us if we wanted to go to Jumbo's afterwards. Meme looked at me, but I knew Mamacita would lose her mind, plus Shellie was with me. We played it off by telling them it was too late to eat.

I was a teen wishing I could hang out. Even though I was young, I should've had more privileges than I did. I was tired of my little tattle-tale sister always hanging out with me. We have a three-year difference between us. Mamacita had made her my security guard. I wanted to run away but I had to put up with the arrangement.

I used to stay out late night without a parent when I was eleven. Now I was being monitored by my sister. It wasn't right. I often screamed. One thing was for sure, I needed my own money. My daddy sent the money to her for me—do I get any? Every now and then, when she felt like being nice. I needed ten dollars and she gave me seven dollars instead. I was upset because I knew darn well that my daddy sent more than twenty dollars.

Summer came and I tried looking for a job. That turned into an impossible feat. I was told Mamacita made too much money. Maybe that was so but I didn't get shit. What the hell did the government know about individual households? They had no clue about mine.

I wanted to do something to make ends. I was not going

to let anyone penny-pinch me, not even Mamacita or my daddy. I'll say it again; looking out for number one was going to be my way of life.

SAY
IT SO!

# 6

Sitting home watching television, Shellie and I heard the news of our life as soon as Mamacita walked in.

"We're moving away?" I asked perplexed.

No, Mamacita didn't come home talking about us moving.

"Come on, let's go see the house."  She said cheerfully while Shellie and I looked at each other like 'what the fuck!'

I wanted to scream on Mamacita like: What the fuck was going on? We were leaving Carol City and going to where? Opalocka? I knew I had to voice my opposition.

"You can't do this to do me.  I don't want to leave."

"Samone, you may not want to but you don't have a choice right now.  You'll see the new place is really much nicer. Furthermore, I already gave the owner the deposit.  That's the end of it."

Damn! I was just starting to get acquainted with the older boys, the big boys getting street money. I had even started selling joints for a dollar at school, building a customer base and making my way. It was happening. Now I have to move. Man, this couldn't be happening.

What was really going on with my plans, my friends, new school, and new boys? Opalocka, starting over that's not a problem, but leaving my new boyfriend is. I knew he'd be calling someone else as soon as I was gone. It always happened just when a boy started cruisin' me. It's something about being Samone.

"Boy oh boy, why must Mamacita play like that?"

The house was cute and the neighborhood was quiet. There was no one outside. I wondered if anyone my age lived in the area. The house had bedrooms far bigger than the ones we had at the old place. There was only one bathroom but the kitchen was spacious. I had a lot of ideas on how to decorate, but Mamacita didn't want to use any of them.

As time moved on, I caught a little more freedom but always felt that any minute things could change.

It got closer to the day we were leaving the old neighborhood for good, and Kevin, my new boyfriend was nowhere to be found. I kept packing and thinking. Man, this life of mine. Boys don't last. My phone rang. I hoped it was him.

"Hello, yes this is Samone speaking," I answered. "Kevin..." I felt better when I heard him.

"Of course I do! Kevin what's up, baby? Ooh! I'm soo glad you called. I'm moving somewhere in Opalocka. For real. Your grandmother lives close. Oh I'm glad I'm moving now. You were locked up? I don't know what was going on for real, but I do know that I'm glad that you called. We're moving next week. Mamacita came out of the blue with this moving shit. All right call me about ten. I'll see if I can steal away for a minute."

Boy, I always cut my plans short for Kevin; that's my baby. Sexy chocolate, double gold in his mouth. He was a sexy ass man.

# 7 STARTING ALL OVER

We moved into the new house, and Shellie, my brat sister immediately started to complain. I didn't know anyone and was bored but was forbidden to go out. Shellie whined. I watched TV and snacked. She'd join me. Soon we all gained weight.

"Samone, see if Meme wants to spend the night, Mamacita said she could." Shellie yelled through the bathroom door.

I was in there, naked checking out my figure. Everything was in the right place. This shortie was stacked.

"I'd rather go over to her house so I can go to the Super Star's roller tech." I shouted back stepping into the shower.

"No way you're gonna leave me in here by myself," Shellie said.

"Oh well..." I was about to start the shower when I heard her.

"No, I'm going to want to go then you know; Mamacita is going to say, 'Shellie can't stay in the house by herself while I'm at work.'"

"You make me sick, you always starting something.  I can't stand your ass." I said.

"All right, if ya'll stay over here, I won't start nothing this weekend.  Ya heard me? Go over Meme's house Friday, all right?"

"Let me call Meme."  I answered.

Friday when Meme came over, she immediately wanted to go outside.

"Hey Shellie, let's go walking," she said.

"Meme loves to walk," Shellie said.

"Your fat butt should walk.  Are you going or are you going to call Mamacita and tell?"

"I'm going walking."

Meme, Shellie and I toured the neighborhood.  We saw several clubs and clothing stores.

"You know the 22nd Avenue players live in this neighborhood?" Meme said.

"Really...?" I asked.

"Dag, Samone, you didn't know that?" Shellie asked.

"Oh, that's right you're so into your boy, Kevin."  Meme said winking.

"Yeah, but I still want to be down."

"Look, there go some boys."  Meme pointed.

If looks could kill, Shellie would have fallen to the floor and busted her head wide open.  By the time we were ready to respond, they were on us.

"Hi…"

"Do ya'll live around here?"

"My cousins have just moved in." Meme said. "What's your name?"

"Maurice, what's yours?"

"I'm Meme, and this is Samone and Shellie."

"Where y'all going?"

"We're just walking, if it's all right with you."

"Who is that cutie?"

"Samone, hmm, hold up, man. I'm walking too." One of the boys chimed in.

By the time we circled the area and got back to the house, we knew the boys' names. We also knew the school Maurice and Vincent attended. They made money from cutting grass. We were standing outside our new home.

"Dag, ya'll need ya'll grass cut." Vincent said.

"You want to cut it? How much do you charge?"

"Twenty-five, for you," he answered.

"Man, do you see that big behind yard?" Maurice said.

"Let me call my mother and see." I said.

We went inside and I dialed her job number.

"May I speak to Yvette Johnson please?" I waited.

"Ma, this boy named Vincent wanted to know if you want your grass cut."

"She said when she gets off work. Come back about six-thirty, all right."

"See ya'll later."

"Oh, give us your number," Maurice said.

I did and they left.

"Maurice is cute, got a little body too, girl, you know he's an athlete."

"Yeah, girl, Vincent is a little chocolate pudding."

"Samone, you love the dark-skinned boys" Meme said.

"Yes girl!" I shouted and smiled.

I liked having company. Mamacita's attitude changed. I remember the time she came home from work and the house wasn't to her satisfaction. Boy -oh- boy, she had the nerve to curse.

"Sometimes I just hate to come home. Ya'll didn't do this, ya'll didn't do that, I'm tired of ya'll half doing stuff."

She was talking about the dirty clothes. I thought to myself, ever since we left Carol City, I've been washing my clothes by hand. Going to the laundramat became a damn privilege. She washed her bloomy soups out by hand. She was lost at parenting. She never taught us how to wash our clothes out by hand. Thank God for common sense.

Shellie was in her own world wondering what was going on. I walked out and hung the wet clothes on the fence. She never warned us about the drastic changes. All she did was yell.

"Your head should be in the books—not in the skating rink."

All of a sudden, Mamacita was trying to change. It was a little too late. I was fourteen and changes had to be made. This house felt wicked. Maybe there were evil spirits in the house. If there were I knew they were working against Mamacita and me. Something wasn't right.

"Samone, Maurice and Vincent are back. Mamacita is outside, laughing and talking with them," Shellie shouted.

"I'm glad they got started, it looks like wild safari back there." I said walking to the window where Shellie stood watching.

"I know," Shellie said.

We sat in the living room and just as Shellie reached for the remote, Mamacita walked in with a drink in her hand.

"I told them fellas that I'll give them fifty dollars." Mamacita said.

"That is a little low," Shellie said.

"Too low? That's embarrassing," I added.

"Time's hard and that's all I've got after y'all eat me out of house and home."

"I guess."

Mamacita sipped her drink and walked away.  Meme joined me and Shellie gazing at the boys from the big window.

"Vincent should be calling us about eleven," Meme said.

"Both of them will be calling?" I asked.

"I'm going to tell.  I want to have company too." Shellie blurted out.

"Damn, you're hot or what? When they call, just get your beggin' ass on the phone and ask," I said.

"Samone, you're not going to ask for me?" Shellie asked.

"Hell no, you're gonna have to put your own rap down, sis."

"I'll ask Maurice for you Shellie," Meme said.

Later that evening Vincent called and it was arranged. The same three came.  Maurice and Vincent brought Ryan to keep

Shellie occupied.  Everything was going according to plan when suddenly Ryan approached Maurice.

"Man, that's a lil' girl.  She's cute an' all, but she need to call me in three more years."  He was out.

After Ryan left we all busted out laughing.  Everybody thought it was funny, except Shellie.  Her lips were shut tight and poked out.  She watched and didn't say anything.  We played games, ate and listened to music.  Then with smiles on our faces, we cleaned up.  It was a good day.

The next thing we knew, Mamacita came through the door.

"What little boys you had in my house?"

We looked at each other like: "Oh shit."

"Samone and Shellie, you know better.  No company when I'm not home, and that goes for you also Meme, because I'm almost quite sure that your mother don't play that."

Shellie and I tried everything not to laugh.  The boys sneaked out when Mamacita turned to walk away.  Then the three of us held a meeting and decided that the next time we had company, we would bring them through the back door.  Our neighbors were being nosy and Mamacita was hardly ever around the back.

# 8

NEW
SCHOOL

School was about to start in a couple of weeks. Shellie would be going to Westview Elementary, and I was going to Westview Junior High. Mamacita was always trying me but I was not having it. I was not planning on going to the new school with no new school clothes. She tried the same thing last year then took Shellie shopping. Just because I didn't come home early from spending the night out, I missed out. I knew she didn't want to take me anyway.

This year it wasn't happening. Shellie and I discussed that we had not been school shopping. I told Shellie I was not going to school if I didn't get any new clothes.

When Mamacita came home, I asked her about shopping. She began explaining and ended with she didn't know. I was angry and couldn't hold back anymore so I started running off my mouth.

"If I don't get any clothes, I'm not gonna go."

"Me either," Shellie said.

I could not believe that Mamacita did not let me have it. She did not say one word. She remembered last school term. The next day, Mamacita called from work.

"You and Shellie get ready. When I come home from work we go."

We did and we got a few outfits for school. I was very satisfied. Now I could mix my old with my new. The 163rd Street shopping center was working. You always find cute things in there. First day of school, Shellie and I left out stalking looking nice. We were glad to go to school with new clothes.

On our way, Shellie and I ran into some girls from the neighborhood. They immediately wanted to know if we had just moved into the house around the corner.

"Yes," we answered.

Nel and Sherry were sisters. Nel went to the junior high and Sherry went to elementary.

"A man had died in that house," Nel said. I was totally convinced that our new home was spooked.

When we got to school, Nel introduced me to Rene who lived on 22nd Avenue. Just so happened, she was in my homeroom.

Later that day, Nel stopped by and introduced me to everyone. It was the start to new friendships. The girls liked to hang at Super Star's roller tech. That was the spot. Seventy Ninth Street was even closer and only a bus ride away. Mamacita would give her permission. Of course she had to show her control.

"If you're not home by twelve, you can't go," she said when I asked her about going.

"The party is just getting started by twelve," I countered.

"How are you getting there? And, I'm not giving you any money."

I knew the saying, and she really didn't want me to go in the first place, so I knew what to do each and every time—I had a lie. I gave her the excuse about Meme's mother. I called from the pay phone.

"Hello, Ma."

"What Samone?"

"Meme's mother is playing cards and she said she won't be able to pick us up until one-thirty."

"Okay," she answered.

My scheme worked every time. I had to get my groove on. Space Funk was jamming, as usual. I was having a great time, but just thinking about Mamacita with all the restrictions made me sad. I wanted to get away from all the favoritism shown to Shellie. I wanted to run away.

When we lived in Carol City I never had to be home before the skating rink closed. The skating rink was closed and Meme and I did not have a ride.

"Come on, Samone, let's go and try to find a ride," Meme suggested.

We did our usual fake stand at the bus stop and waited on some sucker to come along. We were in for a treat. A dude in a green Nova, with the Smurf song playing really loud stopped.

"You girls need a ride?" he asked.

No sooner had Meme and I hopped in than we burst out laughing.

"What was so funny?" He asked.

His bifocals were really thick, but I couldn't tell him so I made up some lame excuse.

"Do you smoke weed?" I asked.  He pulled out a joint. Meme and I smiled.

"Ya'll like feeling good?" he asked lighting up.

"Can you drop us off at the all night store on 22nd Avenue?" I knew we were going to have the munchies.

"Ya'll sure ya'll don't need a lift any further?" he smiled in a nerdy way.

"No," we both replied quickly.

The door locks clicked in position and he had that same smile.

"I'll take you ladies anywhere y'all want to go.  Just say the word," he grinned.

"No this is as far as we want to go.  Thank you." I feigned a smile.

He waited a few minutes then opened the door and let us out of the car.  We hurried into the store.  When we looked outside we saw him still waiting.

"Samone look, that punk is still out there."

"Let's wait a few more minutes.  That pervert must think he's going to get him some ass." I replied.

He finally drove off.  We waited a few minutes then we walked up the street, high and still laughing, talking about how ugly he was.

"He had the nerve to wear them thick-ass glasses, looking like a damn frog, with that big as green Nova looks like a lily pad." I laughed.

Meme busted out in laughter.

"I was thinking the same thing, except I was calling him Kermit the Frog."

We were still in good spirits when we arrived at her home. Meme was the first into her home. I walked around the corner. Mamacita was in the bedroom yelling on the top of her voice.

"I thought you said one- o'clock, Miss Samone."

"Yeah I did." It was just after one-thirty when I arrived home.

"Okay, don't ask to go anymore."

She made me sick, I thought. The battle of the Deejays was scheduled for next week. I'm going; I didn't care. I'll spend the night at Meme's and it would be all good. Meme's mother loved me. I used to go over thereall the time and her mother always made me feel welcome.

Sunday morning I awoke late to the smell of Mamacita's cooking. Fried chicken sure smelled good and greens. On Sunday, I'm in bed until the food was ready so she couldn't make us go to church. Dinner would be ready by twelve or one so back off to sleep I'd go. I woke up about twelve-thirty washed my face, brushed my teeth, and inquired what had been cooked.

"Greens, pigeon peas and rice, oxtails, fried chicken and corn bread," Mamacita said.

I went straight to the pots, fixed my plate ate, ate some

more then went back to sleep. I called Meme and told her to call Mamacita on Wednesday. Mamacita never denied Meme anything. Meme's mother's doors were always open to me.

Sunday evening I knew we were going Over Town and that was always exciting. Meme called and asked what I was doing and said they were jamming on 22nd Avenue at the Johnson brothers' car wash, and asked me if I wanted to go.

"You know it." I answered.

Kevin is probably down there. I jumped into the tub, asked if I could go outside. Everybody was out, people from Carol City, a couple of dudes from the skating rink last night. We got our jam on. I wasn't thinking about Kevin, then, I saw them. Meme and I were smoking. I saw both of Kevin's brothers and this cute, chocolate dude, they were with. Damn!

I don't know what's up in Miami, but these dark-skinned brothers have some smooth, soft skin, no bumps—and fine ass shit. They came over and passed the joint. We were so high, I knew I couldn't go home. I was sailing smooth music playing the Smurf song again. Meme and I bust out laughing. Man, I love the way the fellas dance. They would be grinding and every beat was to perfection.

Northwestern, Carol City, they be getting it krunk. One thing about Dade County, it's live. There was always somewhere to go and stay out late. I was always getting into trouble. Each time I stayed out past my curfew, I'd go home thinking that Mamacita was going to lose it on me.

"What time is it?" I asked Meme.

"Six-thirty," she answered.

"Okay, you want to leave by Seven thirty?"

"Yeah, I don't want ol' girl tripping."

"Okay child, you know how Mamacita plays switch up at any given time. I hate to leave when everybody's dancing and the Ghetto Funk Deejays getting busy."

"Meme you know the battle of the Deejays is this Saturday at the Super Stars."

"I know, Samone. Let's go home."

Meme and I stopped at the store. She always was buying strawberry cookies.

"I'd like a hot sausage please, and a pineapple soda. Meme, you don't have any perfume in your purse?"

"I have this sample of Charlie."

"Okay, it will do."

"Your eyes are red, Samone."

"Shoot, I'll get past that. When we lived on 183rd, old girl used to watch me like a hawk."

"Really, she was like that?" Meme asked.

"She would stare at me and say 'I hope you're not smoking that stuff'." I said and Meme laughed. "One day she had the nerve to smell me. Talking about she knows I'm smoking and don't let me catch you smoking that reefer, girl."

"Samone, I like when you tell your stories, because before you know it, we're home. Dag, it's just seven-fifteen. I know they're going to think that we bumped our heads. Meme said.

"Right, call you later, okay." I said.

Damn, let me get myself together. I thought as I walked home.

"Mamacita's got company." Shellie informed.

I was about to ask whom when I heard a voice.

"Hi, Samone…"

"Hi, Paula…"

"What, you came in early?"

"Yeah, I got to get ready for school tomorrow."

"You sick or sump'n?"

"I'm fine."

I knew she would be trying to show-off, being over polite and all.

"You're not…"

"No, Mamacita I just got to use the bathroom." I said running off. She was making me nervous. I was looking in the mirror thinking she might be trying to play some type of trick on me. I climbed into the tub and brushed my teeth.

"Samone…"

"Huh…"

"Nel called and asked if you can come over next weekend. I told her you were the one with the busy weekend schedule and it was up to you."

You know I was standing there wearing nothing but a big smile on my face.

"Okay…"

"So, call her when you get out of the tub. Ya heard me?"

"Okay…"

"You want me to fix you a plate?" she asked.

"Yes, thank you, Mamacita." I answered.

I love it when Paula came over; Mamacita acted so nice. I

thought as I dialed.

"Nel, what's up?"

"Samone, I called Mamacita, she said it was up to you."

"I know thanks. She told me."

"So, clean up the house. Don't make her mad, whatever she takes out for dinner, you cook it." Nel warned.

"I'll do just that. You know she loves when I surprise her. The first thing she says is, 'I'm so glad that I don't have to come home and cook today.'"

We both laughed. I hung up the phone and joined my family for dinner.

# 9

"Shellie time to get up," I said shaking my sister and walking away. "Monday morning time to get a fresh start. Dag, ya'll must've had a long weekend. Mamacita, it's time for you to get up. Rise and shine." I was on a roll. Mamacita looked at me and busted out laughing.

"You couldn't wait to get me with my own words, huh?"

Everything went according to plan. After school, I cooked the Lamb chops that Mamacita left out. By Thursday morning, I had a little stash from saving my lunch money all week. I was prepared just in case Mamacita tried to hit me with her usual, 'I don't have any extra money' routine.

I had also helped Nel's mother and she gave me thirty dollars. I was straight. I couldn't help but be happy when Friday rolled around, time to move my feet.

"Samone, Meme's at the door." Shellie announced.

"What's up, Meme?"

"Nothing, you ready?"

"Yeah, let me grab my books."

"Girl, the ol' girl's tripping. Her and her man at it," Meme said with a frown.

"Damn, girl!"

"I don't know if I'm going to be able to go." Meme said as we walked outside.

"What about you, you straight?"

"So far, so good," I answered with fingers crossed.

"That makes one of us..."

"Yeah, Paula was over this week. Mamacita was chill."

"I wish my mother's boyfriend would act right."

"I cooked yesterday." I said.

"Oh you're really getting her ready, huh?"

"You know it. Plus, I cleaned up and vacuumed every day. You'd think I could get a break, but of course not."

"I gotta get some help. I hope her and her man make up quick."

"Shoot, help them, girl. Fry some fish when you get home. You know your mother and her boyfriend loves them some fried-fish Friday evenings. Try that."

That evening I had finished frying fish and was sitting back watching TV, waiting for the cornbread to bake.

"Samone," Mamacita called.

"Yes, Mamacita," I answered.

"Here's thirty dollars."

"Thanks," I said and almost fainted.

"What's that look for girl? Your daddy sent some money. You can go up to the Flea Market and get you a couple of things."

"Thank you, Mamacita." I said and walked away calculating.

Meme and I could get a three-dollar bag of weed. Then we could stop over Nel's house and smoke.

Saturday morning, I got up. Meme called to let me know that her mother and stepfather were still in bed watching TV. Judging from the moaning and groaning coming from their bedroom, watching TV was not all they were doing.

"Mamacita's busy making breakfast for us and Paula's still here. Everything was working out well."

I smiled showered, and was getting ready to meet Meme as planned.

"Ya'll grab a bowl of cereal before ya'll go to the Flea Market. Ya'll think ya'll going to look cute."

I did and was out before Shellie could get ready. I had to ditch her and ducked out real fast.

"Samone, what're you getting?" Meme asked when we met outside the candy store.

"I don't know, probably some Jordache. They always look real good on me."

"Hmm..."

"Girl, all I know is I'm going to have me some fun."

"Samone, you want to get another three-cent bag?"

We both bought two pairs of jeans, and matching tops. We always had some type of shoes to match our outfits, so that was never a problem.

"Same routine as Friday, except the Super Star's roller tech, baby." We smiled at each other after getting dressed.

"Ya'll two again?" The weed man said when we returned to cop.

"Super Stars," Meme exclaimed.

"I was thinking about going to that myself, for real?"

"Samone, it's six o'clock; lets go home about seven eat, take our baths, and let that crazy-ass brother of mine drop us off." Meme suggested.

"I can't wait for tonight. Space Funk is going to crush Ghetto Style."

"You know it, Space Funk deejays are the world's greatest!" Meme agreed.

When we arrived at Nel's house, we could hear her singing the lyrics to Tina Marie and Rick James; *Fire and Desire.* Meme and I walked in singing along.

*Love me tender... you are my fire and desire...*

"What's up lil' sis?" Nel greeted us at the door.

"Hey girl," we answered and pulled out the two bags of weed.

"Oh...oh...I see y'all ready." Nel smiled.

"Give us some perfume and let me brush my teeth." I said.

"Damn, Samone, you have a toothbrush everywhere you go." Meme said as she sparked a joint, puffed twice then passed it.

"That's right. I may have left Carol City, but not my toothbrushes." I said taking the joint and puffing hard.

"Samone, you said that like you were in the US Army, all at attention and shit." Nel laughed started the giggles.

"You and Meme is high as hell."

"That's right, Samone." Meme said.

"It's time to get krunk and tear up that house. We will definitely be the center of attention."

"Off to the races." We chorused.

We left Nel's laughing and feeling really good.

Space Funk was jamming as usual. The fellas from Liberty City were all over the place. The Northwestern crew represented. The atomic dog was pumping; the Northwestern crew got busy chasing the cat. They were on the floor in push-up style, with one leg up, the other down and humping to the music. They were barking loud jumping over one another.

*Bow, wow, wow, yippy yo, yippy ya yeah...*

Super Stars was off the chains and I was having fun sweating and dancing wildly with the boys tonight. Meme and Nel were enjoying themselves.

"Samone, you see the Northwestern boys? Did they make it live as fuck up in here or what?" Meme asked while looking around.

"Yeah girl, it's live, live, live up in here." I shouted over the loud music.

"Samone is that Kevin dancing over there? And he's with a white girl."

"Yep, I see them, girl. Whew, Kevin's lucky that's his friend girl. Or else!"

"C'mon Nel, I'm going to introduce him. All that gold look

good in their mouths. Look at Kevin with his cute black self." I said.

All I know was that night Kevin made all the right moves. We danced, hugged and he bought me drinks.

That night we disappeared in his ride and went to his crib and he made sweet love to me. Yeah, I had that smooth, black complexion brother in me. He went easy and made it smooth that first time. I ached for him to fill me up. All night long calling my name while kissing my lips.

Later he took me back to the party where my girls were still having fun.

DO THE
OVER TOWN
BREAK-DOWN

# 10

"Mom..."

"What Nel?"

"The phone..."

"Tell whoever it is that I'm in the bathroom."

"It's your man.  He said if you're coming? They're jamming under the bridge."

"All right, ya'll get ready, ya'll lil' hot asses ain't tired yet?"

"Mom, we're having too much fun."  Nel answered.

"Oh yes!"

"Samone..."

"Yes..."

"You said that?"

"You know it."

Nel, Meme and I busted out laughing.  I hate to go home

it was so much love over here at Nel's house.

"Samone, where is your mind girl?" Meme asked.

"Who's talking? You look spaced out." I said.

"You're still high from last night." Meme said.

"Okay, damn, I'm in a daze for real." I said walking on shaky legs.

"Go get in the shower and snap out of it."

"Girl, if you could have seen your expression." Nel laughed.

"Damn, it's that bad? Let me go jump in the shower."

I came out later and the radio was on full blast.

"Samone, you hear the music?" Meme asked.

"*Do the over town break down.*" Nel chanted, dancing along to the song.

"Where you want me to drop ya'll off at?" Nel's mother asked.

"Are you going cross town?" Nel asked.

"Yeah, I'll probably pick your grandmother up first, cause dinner will start at seven, and ya'll walk ya'll lil' butts right up the street. I'll take you home about ten, Samone."

"Okay..."

*Do the over town break down...*

We all got in the car and Nel's mother drove off with us still singing.

"Man, this weekend been straight fun." Meme said.

"Right back to school tomorrow," Nel said.

"True, is that right Samone?" Meme smiled.

"That's right, but we can party at two jams in Over Town

before we go."

*Do the over town break down...*

"What's up Meme?" I said glancing at her.

"Samone, are you hanging?" Meme asked.

Nel's mother let us off and we walked to the entrance of the dance.

"What're you thinking, girl?" Meme asked.

"I told ol' girl I'll be back early." I answered.

"Okay, who are you up here with?" Meme asked.

"Nel and you," I smiled.

"Nel...?"

"She's with her mother and they're cool."

"That's the story you'll give. Just call and tell her you're gonna be late."

Meme went to use the pay phone and returned with a smile.

"She's relaxing with her man. And you know he just got back from vacation."

"He's wearing that out." Nel laughed.

"Hmm, hmm... Amen." I said.

"I hope he gets her in all the positions." Meme laughed. "She'll be dead tired by the time I get in."

We went into the party and had some more fun until Nel's mother came and took us home.

*Do the Over town break down...*

We all sang, laughed and broke out doing the dance.

After that, we went with Nel's mother to eat. Fried chicken, stewed conch, collard greens, cabbage greens, corn bread, pigeon peas and rice, ice tea, buffet style were set up buffet-style. We washed our hands, blessed the table and ate. The food was delicious. Nothing quenched like a good glass of ice-tea.

"Oh God, it's ten-thirty let me get you home, Samone."

We piled into the car and she drove as fast as possible the short blocks.

"All right, goodnight everybody." I said.

"Goodnight Samone."

"Dag, the fun is over; back to the drawing board." I said to Meme as we parted company.

"Goodnight, Meme."

"Goodnight, Samone."

"Dag, it seems like you got me here in fifteen minutes."

"Yeah..."

As soon as I was in the house, Mamacita was up in arms, yelling.

"Don't you dare ask to go over there anytime soon. It's eleven o' clock. I hope you've eaten because I put the food up."

"I used to have dinner every Sunday with Meme her family and you never fuss when they bought me home late like this when we used to live on a 183rd."

"Well, you can all sing next Sunday in church."

"Man!"

"Man nothing. You're going, you've been out two weeks straight and I haven't said a word to you about it."

Don't get me wrong I loved church, I've been in church forever —Church of God and Christ—loved it. After Sunday school we'd eat. But you needed money, because hamburgers, jumbo hotdogs, hot sausage, pickled pig's feet, sodas, and donuts cost money. You have to eat since church started at one in the afternoon.

"I can't wait until I'm grown and able to leave."

"Then you'll wish you were young again. Goodnight Samone. I don't want to hear another word out of you."

The next morning I was tired but was out in front of the school before Nel arrived.

"Damn, she better hurry or she'll be late for school." Meme said. "Nel and her sister are always running late."

"Hi ya'll."

"How're you doing?"

"I'm fine girl, nice to see you."

"Same here..."

# 11

THAT IS
HOW IT IS

Mamacita started blowing me up. She wasn't feeling well and was home from work one day when Kevin stopped by. Mamacita went on the warpath.

"I don't want you to take company until you are sixteen."

"But Mamacita I had boyfriend…"

"And don't forget what they're capable of. Turn around and your hot ass is pregnant again. We can't afford another mouth right now."

"But Mamacita it's not like that…"

"This is what you do when I'm at work, Samone?"

"No Mamacita, I go to school."

"Don't let them lil' boys get you in trouble. You hear me?"

"Yes Mamacita."

She cock-blocked by lying on the sofa the whole time

Kevin was there.  Her mannish-ass made me so sick I could vomit.

"I guess your mom isn't going anywhere," Kevin whispered.

He and I had been sitting in front of the TV for about an hour.  There were no kisses and no hugs.  I wanted to but could not touch him until we walked to the bus stop.

We shared a hug and a light kiss.  Kevin was the type that did not want his business all over the street.  His philosophy was that if a dude didn't have anywhere to take his girl, then he should hold her hand, go for a walk and always respect her when you were on the streets.  Kevin kissed me and got on the bus.  I walked down the street and ran into Nel and her sister.

"Hey Samone, what you fittin' to get into?" they greeted.

"Heading home..."

"We're on our way to the U-Todum.  Wanna come along?"

"I better not, Kevin just left; ol' girl is home acting crabby."

"Damn I could tell something was up, you look out of it." Nel said.

"Yeah, the same ol' shit...I can't wait till it's over."

"She's cock-blocking?"

"Yep and I'm sick of the shit.  Ol' girl stays home and fucks up my whole evening.  Damn, I can't wait till I'm grown."

"All mothers are crazy!"

We stood silent, quiet as a mouse.  I walked with them not saying a word.  After that day, everything was different.  I started looking at my living quarters, kept washing clothes by hand, using the laundry when I could.  Things were worse.  Mamacita was drinking a lot and when the alcohol kicked in, there was no telling how she would act.

Then she started getting sicker and would only take care of herself when Paula came over. Mamacita would wear a smile all weekend long.

STILL
MEETING
PEOPLE

# 12

Nel, and I walked to school and she bought a new friendly face as usual.

"Samone," she said. "This is Tasha. Tasha, Samone."

"Hello, Samone," the smiling girl said. She seemed too old even for high school. It really didn't matter. I'd treat her like another face in the crowd.

"Hello, Tasha."

When we reached the cafeteria someone yelled.

"Tasha, Tasha!"

We were looking around. It was this skinny girl with orange hair, looking between the fence-poles.

"Yolanda is that you?" Tasha asked.

"What's up girl? Where you been?"

They were really happy to see one another.

Yolanda introduced us to some of her friends.

"Hi, how're you doing Samone? It's nice to see you again Nel." Yolanda said. She was shapely, attractive and wore make-up like a model.

"Hey Yolanda," both Nel and I said. We all laughed.

"Let's have a slumber party over at my house this Saturday." Tasha suggested. "Samone, you're more than welcome."

"Okay, sounds good. See y'all later." I answered getting away quickly.

We all headed to our homerooms. I made it my business not to ask Nel about Tasha or Yolanda. I didn't want the gossiping thing beginning. I had too many fights in Carol City from that kind of bullshit. I definitely didn't want history repeating itself.

To avoid the drama, I walked home alone, changed into my white tennis shorts and my yellow gator shirt. I heard knocking at the door. To my surprise there was Kevin. He looked down at my shorts and shook his head.

"I hope you didn't go to school in those tight ass shorts."

"No, I just put them on for you baby."

"Well, you might as well take them off."

"Why?"

"Didn't you just hear me, Samone, they are too damn tight. Find another pair."

I loved it when Kevin gave me any type of attention.

"Think you're gonna keep wearing them when I ain't around? Bring them here."

"For what...?"

"Those are going in the trash."

"Dag!" I said wiggling out my favorite pair of shorts.

"Dag nothing," he said promptly throwing my fucking show stopper shorts in the damn trash.

"You might as well straighten your face up, girl."

As soon as we started kissing, Shellie knocked.

"Hi Kevin...I'm going right back outside. We're about to go hang. I'll see you later, Samone. I'll be back before the old girl gets home."

"Hey Shellie, here's couple a dollars."

"Thanks Kevin."

"What has Samone been up to?" Kevin asked handing her the money.

"Smoking weed and hanging out that's about it." Shellie said.

"Yeah, that's right. Bye Shellie." I said.

"Yeah, I've been hearing that yo lil' ass on the regular is hanging all Over Town."

"That's right."

"You like that huh?" He asked sounding jealous.

"This fine ass must be seen..." I said rubbing my hands over my butt.

Kevin grabbed me and started kissing me hard on my lips. He nibbled on my neck leaving passion marks. Then he pulled my panties down. I put up weak resistance. His lust drove him wild. It felt good, but I wasn't ready for this. He ripped my thighs opened and mounted me. We fucked for an hour. When he left, I went right in the trash and got my shorts. He must be crazy. I was going to wear my shorts until I can't button them anymore. I walked over to Meme's house and told her what happened.

"I know you went and got them out the trash; you love them more than weed." She laughed.

"Child, I'm going back in the house, so when ol' girl comes home I can ask her about Tasha's slumber party before she makes plans for me to go to church. I hope her ass have some company like Paula."

"All right later." Meme said.

"Samone, Mamacita called and said she was going to be running late. She said you can cook if you want to. She said that she left the steak out. Cook, Samone. Please." Shellie pleaded.

"All right you vacuum the floor, and I'll wash the dishes."

"Where the hell are you trying to go this weekend, Samone?"

"This girl name Tasha, is having a slumber party she lives by the Crab House, looks like Little House on the Prairie, one house and all that land."

"Girl, you got a passion mark on your neck."

"I know."

"You better not let Mamacita see it."

"She never does." I said and began dealing with the cooking chores.

After Shellie and I ate we were tired of waiting and went back out. Mamacita was taking too long and everybody was outside. All the older girls were hanging at the bus stop trying to get a boyfriend with a car. The fellas stopped most of the time for Meme and me. Then we'd go riding, smoke weed and drink Private Stock.

One time these boys took us to the beach. After that they wanted us to go over their house. I made up a story and they dropped us off at the U-Todum. We hung out and chilled as usual. Then our lil' sisters popped up, saw us getting out of the car and started talking about telling on us.

I knew Shellie would tell, but not right away. She was going to blackmail me. Then I'd enjoyed whipping her ass. Nel's lil' sister went right around the corner and snitched. Her mother told her to leave the bus stop and come home immediately. She got put on a week's punishment.

That evening I was home watching Mamacita enjoying the food.

"That steak was really good." Mamacita said licking her lips.

"Ma, could I stay over this girl named Tasha's house?"

"Who is Tasha?"

"She lives by the U-tom, and she's having a slumber party and all the girls supposed to spend the night."

"Samone, don't keep thinking you're going out of here every weekend. Make this your last one. And your phone has been ringing off the hook."

"Probably for Shellie," I said without checking.

"The phone rings more for you than her."

"That's not my fault."

"There it goes again. I bet you it's for you."

"Hello, what's up?"

"It's for you, right?"

"Yep..."

"Just what I told you," Mamacita said and walked away.

"Hello, Meme..." I said answering the phone. "It's the old girl. She's been complaining that the phone was ringing off the hook. Oh yeah, this weekend...? I'm staying over Tasha's house at her slumber party...Kevin told you his friend was checking you out on the avenue...? When...? For real at the car wash...Saturday? Oh yeah, that's good. We could waste half the day and go over Tasha's house and eat her food up, cause her fat ass love to eat. Later girl," I said and hung the phone.

The weekend came and went so fast, it made my head spin. Kevin had me in that hot-ass back room, trying to pound my lil' coochie out. He didn't even know my real age. All he knew was; I went to the junior high. I kept him chasing me until he was tired. I know one day he was going to get really tired of my shit, but until then, so be it.

Whew! What a slumber party. We ate listened to music and after that, the usual girl chit-chat. Monday morning came quickly. I went outside and felt the winds and knew Thanksgiving was on its way.

"Ma, don't we have to go to church this Sunday?" Shellie woke up perky and yelling.

I looked at her wearing her devilish grin and thought 'you little bitch'. What trip was she on? I hurried up and got dressed for school, because I knew this lil' bitch was riding her broom. I didn't want to wild out on her and give her one of those vicious ass whippings she's probably trying to church up on. I was getting dressed when the lil' bitch yelled.

"Ma, Samone is trying to leave me."

"Samone, you're not going to wait for Shellie?"

"I haven't been waiting lately. She walks with her friends and I walk with mine. What's the big deal today?"

"She wants to walk with her big sister; wait for her." Mamacita laughed and said.

These two got some shit with them. I waited, but when we were out the front door; I left her ass and began walking very fast.

"Samone," Nel yelled.

"What!"

"What's wrong with you?" Nel asked.

"That nosy-ass sister of mine, stay trying it. All of a sudden this morning, she wants someone to walk her fat ass. I'm a give her a fat lip any minute now."

"Yeah, I feel you. My lil' sister give me hell all the time."

"Nel, she pushes my buttons. Shellie knows that I will fuck her up. I can't wait for lunch."

"Damn, Samone, we haven't had breakfast yet." Nel said.

"I know. Was that the bell for homeroom?"

"Yep..."

"What time is it?"

"Eight thirty-five."

"Where did time go girl, everybody's running late this morning?"

"I know, we didn't get to eat breakfast."

"Nel, your ass can eat, but you do maintain that weight."

On my way to homeroom I saw Meme.

"Okay, Meme what's wrong with your face, girl?" I asked.

"Tasha tried me. The bitch just started speaking badly about me. I told that ho' we can see each other after school. Samone you and Nel know how spoiled her ass is. And she had the nerve to say since Samone moved in the neighborhood, I don't come over her house that much. I asked her how the fuck she figures; we just started back speaking."

"What's up ya'll?" Yolanda said joining us.

"Damn, Meme what's wrong with your face?" Yolanda asked.

"That bitch Tasha trying it again."

"See, she don't know me or Samone. I'll punch that bitch in her face off the top." Meme said.

"Really I didn't know..." Yolanda started but I cut her off.

"After school I'm down for mine. I know we just met and I spent the night over her house and everything, but I don't play putting my name in simple shit."

Miraculously, Tasha was absent from lunchroom. I knew the phony bitch was on a guilt trip. I already had an attitude from the morning and taking my frustrations out on someone was all right by me.

"Let's get off of the school grounds because they will get us for that."

Three o'clock came and all four of us met on 22nd Avenue.

"She is going to pick her little brother up first, and I don't want to fight her by my house." Meme said.

"Damn, Meme," Nel said.

"Let's meet her by the record store." Meme suggested.

That's what we did. When she got there, I approached Tasha.

"I don't have time for y'all lil' girl's games," I said.

"Shit, that shit you said earlier to Meme was that lil' girl's games?"

"Just keep my name out your mouth." I said.

She was holding an umbrella and pointed it in my face.

"Samone, your name ain't shit, bitch."

I threw my right fist in her face. She swung the umbrella. I ducked. Yolanda sucker punched her. She turned and Meme hit her in the head. Her brother started crying and he almost ran into the street. Tasha started wildly throwing blows. She swung the umbrella and I grabbed it. I started wrestling her big ass for the umbrella. I was stronger and after awhile, I got real mad and snatched it away.

"Give me this damn umbrella."

"Please don't hit my sister." Her brother cried.

We stopped and stared at him. His voice reminded me of when Shellie's father and Mamacita used to fight. All I could hear was my grandmother begging him not to hit her anymore. Tasha grabbed him and the fight was over. The crowd was hyped. We all were telling our part.

"Meme what was you doing, a hit and run? You ran up

then ran back." Yolanda was laughing. We all joined in.

"Shit, she had that umbrella. I wasn't going to let her hit me with it." Meme said.

"Samone, you just manhandled her big ass and took the damn thing." Yolanda said.

"I cut my fingers strong arming that ho.'"

We busted out laughing. When I got in the house Shellie was real scared.

"If you put your hands on me, I swear I'm going to tell Mamacita about what happened at the bus stop."

"I'm tired of you and Mamacita."

I left out to avoid having to kick her ass. It was too much fighting. Mamacita would lose it on me. I'd have to defend myself.

"You better come back in here and clean up." I heard Shellie's voice.

"That's all right. I'll take it. But when I get that fat dog, I'm going to get her for all her old and new tricks."

I cleaned up. Meme and Yolanda came over looking scared.

"Samone, girl, Tasha's mother called my mother. My sister answered and told her she'd let my mother know. Tasha's mother will be in school at seven a.m. She's trying to have all the parents meet her there." Yolanda was running her mouth as we walked. I stopped and stared.

"What's wrong, Samone?" Meme asked. Yolanda's mouth and steps halted. They waited for me to catch up. Then Yolanda began to blab away.

"My sister told me ol' girl was pissed off. She mentioned

that you slept-over her house and that you cut Tasha.  She said she was going to press charges against you."

"Whatever! Fuck that, bitch! I snatched the umbrella from her and both of us got cut.  These are my wounds."  I said showing both hands.

"Hmm, hmm.  You definitely got cut too."  Yolanda said.

"Yeah, that's proof enough."  Meme said.

"Plus both of you were there and that's the truth.  Is this girl a liar? If I get in trouble for this I'm going to stick my foot in her fat red ass."

"I'll help you," Meme said.

"She better tell the truth or it's on.  She told her mom I was punching her in the back," Yolanda added.

"Damn right, her fat ass was swinging that umbrella like a maniac."  Meme laughed.

"All three of us were there and we didn't start shit.  She did."  Yolanda said.

"We just did what we had to do," I said.

We gave each other five.  Then we all busted out laughing.

# 13 NEXT MORNING

5:00 am. I woke up and it dawned on me that this would be the day of doom. Mamacita knew nothing but she'd soon find out. I thought of telling her while staring at the ceiling. I should just tell her and save my own soul. I knew she was going to flip the damn script.

"Good morning Mamacita. I got something to tell you," I said sitting down for breakfast.

"Oh Lord, what is it Samone?"

"Yesterday we got into a fight."

"Who's this *we*?"

"Yolanda, Meme, and myself," I answered.

"Oh really, who did y'all three get in a fight with?"

"We...ah...Tasha..."

"The girl whose house you just spent the night over at...?"

"Yes, but she started it…"

"When did this all happen?"

"Yesterday…"

"That's why the school's been trying to get a hold of me?"

"Mamacita, I was defending myself…I…"

"Mamacita, Mamacita…"

"What do you want, Shellie?"

"Tasha is a real big girl and she started just like Samone sez."

I couldn't believe my sister was sticking up for me.

"Is that the truth, Samone?"

"I'm telling the truth."

"That Meme, she's into everything. I told you if you tell the truth I'd stick by you and I will." Mamacita said, her eyes shifting from my face to Shellie's.

"I'm telling the truth. Meme and Yolanda will tell their sides. Our stories are all the same." I said.

"Oh my, look at the time. Come on, y'all got to hurry up and get to school…"

"Mamacita…"

"What now, Samone, more bad news you forgot to tell me?"

"Her mama is going to the school and wants to meet with all the parents."

"No can do. I've got to go to work. You tell them to call me at my job. Now hurry off to school and don't go putting your hands on people's children."

Shellie and I walked out the door. I held her hand and crossed the street with her.

"Thanks," I said as we waited for Nel and her sister.

"Thanks for what?" Shellie asked.

"Oh don't worry about it." I smiled.

"Hey y'all," Nel said walking to us.

"Hi Nel." We both greeted smiling.

"Heard about what happened yesterday?"

"Yes, we did." Shellie and I said. We laughed together.

Damn we didn't even get to homeroom before they called our first and last names.

"Tasha Washington, Nel Blackmon..."

I looked real crazy when they called her name.

"...Samone Johnson, Yolanda King and Meme Hopkins, report to the principal's office immediately."

Everyone was staring at us. They knew what happened. Some gave dirty looks, but I didn't give a fuck. My face was a mean grill and whoever wanted it, could get it. Right now I was at my highest level of piss-tivity. What bothered me was not that the chicken-head had lied, but what was Nel a witness to?

I fumbled with my thoughts as I walked to the office.

"I'm Samone Johnson." I said.

"Oh yes, Samone. Go right into Ms. Walker's office, please. She's expecting you."

The teacher told us to take all our belongings and books as if she knew we were going home. I walked in and saw that everyone was there including both the Principal and the assistant. Tasha and her mother sat together. Meme and Yolanda were there and I was walking over to stand next to them. All of a sudden I glanced at Yolanda then both our eyes locked and stared at Nel. I was trying to send Nel a message. She knew what was going to happen.

"Okay, everyone's here. Let's get going. Now you all know why we're here...?"

The principal spoke and my mouth went dry waiting to tell my side of the story. I stood calmly and listened while Tasha lied. When she had the nerve to say I cut her hand, I butted-in.

"I did not cut you. I snatched the umbrella you were swinging, trying to hit me and my friends."

"Yeah, after my brother started crying and almost ran in the street! Maurice was the one who caught him. Ask him." Tasha yelled.

"Get Maurice in here, ASAP," Principal Walker said.

"Why you wanna see me? I didn't do nothing and whoever call my name I'm see them too!"

You could hear him coming down the hall, talking loud.

"Come in and shut the door, Maurice. You were on the scene yesterday when this..."

"Yeah, but I ain't done nothing..."

"Okay tell me what happened yesterday?"

"I saw the lil' boy fittin' to run across the street and I stopped him. That's all."

"Thank you."

"All right, Nel did you see Samone cut Tasha?"

"No, I..."

"That's all I need to know, thanks Nel. What about you Meme? Did you see..."

"No sir."

"Hmm...Yolanda... What about you?"

"Nope..."

"Maurice?"

"Nah man, that girl just took her umbrella. This fool was swinging all wild I would have tried to take it too. She could've hit lil' man, then he goes running and all that. It was just drama in the street."

"Samone, where is your mother today?" Principal Walker asked.

"She's at work. She said you could call her there."

"Tasha you stated that this incident happened at the record store. It wasn't on school grounds?"

"Yes, sir..."

"You weren't here last year, were you Samone?" the principal asked.

"No, I was at Carol City."

"My uh...Carol City?" The principal mused.

"Yes sir. Your niece and I went to the same Elementary school together there." I answered.

"Oh, you mean Quando...? She's such a sweet girl. Her mother and I are first-cousins...well that's not important." The principal said with an embarrassing smile.

"Yes, you can ask her if she knows Samone Johnson."

"I'll do that, Samone."

Tasha's mother stared bullets at me. I may have needed a vest.

"What do you think?" the principal asked the assistant.

"Firstly, more serious than ever we don't have enough for

police involvement.  All evidence clears Samone Johnson and proves that she did not cut Tasha Smith.  This will go on everyone's school record.  Secondly, there is nothing we can do technically because it didn't happen on school grounds and occurred more than fifty feet away."  The assistant principal, Mr. Lattimore said.

"They didn't have to jump her."  Nel suddenly blurted.

"Meme you Yolanda and Tasha have been friends forever. Why...?"

"Since Samone joined the mix, she's been acting jealous."

"Ms. Hall, give Maurice a pass to his class please.  Samone, we will notify your mother.  Let this be your warning, if I hear anything or see you back in my office for anything, five days outdoor suspension.  Ms. Johnson is that clear?"

"Yes sir."

"And leave these girls alone."

"No problem, sir".

At lunchtime, Meme, Yolanda and I held a group session between us.

"Nel is a fake butt.  She better not say nothing to me."  I said kicking off the powwow.

"The whole damn school is looking shocked.  It's like they can't believe we still in school."  Yolanda said.

"How? Cause we told the truth, that's how."  I said.

Maurice walked over to where we were.

"Samone, you should have beaten that big, red bitch with that umbrella. How she's gonna try and lie? I know it was her fat ass put my name in it.  You're way smaller than her.  She told everybody she was jumped and cut. That's why the whole school is acting like they against you."

"You don't say?"

"I'm telling you, that's why everybody amped-up."

"Damn!"

"Watch out for that big, fat-ass Tracey. She's one of Tasha's friends. She's been asking about you Samone. Be careful, she is with the 22ndAve players."

"I thought that gang was for boys?" I asked.

"It is, but four of her cousins are down with them. My brother is in that shit, that's how I know."

"Hmm..." I pondered the odds.

"Aren't the police investigating them?" Meme asked.

"Yeah that's why they are chilling," Maurice said.

"Damn Samone you'd think that you fuck up ten people, you are going to be popular real soon." Yolanda said.

"Yep in the worse way but whoever trying to see me. Better come hard!" I said.

"I'm with you girl." Meme said.

"How does Tracey look? I wanna be aware when her fat ass jump."

"That's her big ass right there." Yolanda said.

Vincent came over and joined Maurice.

"Y'all are alright?" he asked.

"Yeah, man I ain't scared of none of these hos," I said.

I stayed in that evening and gave thought to the whole swing of things. There were many stories about the 22nd-Avenue players. It was alleged that they have been involved in killings, looting and burning down houses. If it was that serious, they could take it to the next level.

"I can't believe your butt's inside?" Mamacita said as she walked in.

"Yeah," I deadpanned.

"The school called me about your episode. Keep on thinking you're bad; somebody is going to beat your behind. Your mouth is going to get you in trouble. You may have gotten away this time but principal said it's going on your school record that's another strike against you far as college. No one is going to accept you with your record. You're in trouble and school has only been in session for two months. I'm not going to be running back and fourth. You need to get your act together. Leave 'em lil' pisss'n-tail-boys alone, and put something else on your mind."

"I do my work in school and I'm not going to let anyone put their hands on me and think that I'm not going to hit back."

Mamacita stared at me.

"So if I put my hands on you, are you going to hit me back?" she asked.

"No!" I said.

I got up and went to my room. I knew she was trying to start; she'd never be on my side.

I sat in my room thinking about the time Shellie slapped the little boy on the way to school. He walked back home and told his mother I did it. His mother came to the school and slapped me when I walked through the door. I was stunned. Mamacita took her to court. The judge gave her probation. In the end Mamacita withdrew the charges because the woman had children and

Mamacita did not want her to go to jail.

I took a bath and watched TV. I hated to be in the house but I stayed anyway even though I wasn't worried.

"Are you hungry?" Mamacita asked.

"No," I said. I didn't tell her I didn't want her company. I didn't feel like being criticized. The telephone rang.

"Hello, this is Samone. What's up Meme?"

From that day on we rolled together, the three of us, Meme, Yolanda and I.

A week later, Yolanda called me and told me that a girl came around. Some big red tomboy who lived in the corner house, not too far from me, was threatening to beat my ass. Yolanda told me she played basketball like she was a pro and could fight. For the next few weeks all the talk was about her. Her mother sent her to job corps because she kept getting in trouble. She was down with the 22ndAve players. Her name was Sharon.

This girl knew that I was from Carol City and she let everyone know that if I wanted to fight her it would be no problem. Either way she was planning on kicking my ass. Trouble was stalking. One day at school, a girl and I got into it at lunchtime because she was tired of hearing my name.

"You think you're bad huh? It won't take much to whip your lil', short ass," she said.

"Whatever, you big, ugly, gorilla looking bitch!"

"All that bullshit you're talking is gonna get you in a lot of trouble." She warned as she walked away.

After that explosion, I knew she was going to fight me no matter what. I didn't care. Whenever she was ready she'll get a beat down.

That afternoon, three-o-clock took forever to come. When school did let out, I was in for a rude awaking. Nel ran back in the schoolyard.

"The whole 22nd Avenue players are outside with big Tracey. They're looking for y'all," she said excitedly.

"I'll fight her big ass. I'll find out if that big bitch's scared," I said.

We went outside and saw that Nel was right. A pick-up truck filled with niggas along with Sharon and Tracey was parked waiting.

"What's up with you two bitches? Meme, if you step up, you gonna get your ass tore up too." Tracey yelled.

"Whatever you fat bitch!" I yelled and started walking towards them.

"Aw shit! She's a bad-ass bitch. She's coming over here." Sharon said.

"Samone…" Yolanda yelled.

"What?"

"Don't go."

"I'm not scared of her big ass. The bigger they come the harder they fall!" I yelled.

"Oh, she think she all that," Sharon said.

"Bring your big fat funky ass down here big bitch," I said.

Through it all, I heard Yolanda calling me again.

"Samone don't go, they gonna jump you!"

One of the male teachers walked out and began writing our names in his book. Everyone scattered.

"Okay now y'all wanna leave? Stupid big asses," I said.

"That will be, enough cursing Samone." The teacher said and brought me back inside. He called Yolanda and Meme.

Mamacita is going to hit the ceiling, I thought as the teacher spoke to me.

"I need you all to be in the principal's office first thing in the morning. Now go on home ladies. And don't let me have to come looking for you tomorrow morning."

"This trouble all because of that big fat, bitch." I said walking away.

"My mother is going to have a fit and I haven't said shit out of my damn mouth," Meme said.

"Yeah, but if I let big bitch talk and I don't do or say anything but let her big bully-ass try me, she'll keep on testing me," I said.

"You right Samone. Fuck it. A girl got to do what a girl got to do," Meme said.

We started laughing till we were doubled over and our shoulders hunched. Then we walked home to face the music. We spotted fat Tracey alone on the corner and she looked scared. She quickly dipped into Sharon's house. We laughed as her big ass disappeared and never came back out.

"My grandmother always said, 'Get the baddest one out of

the crowd, then you won't have to worry about anyone else's," I said.

A car came by with loud music blasting. We started dancing, laughing and doing the whip. Finally, big Tracey came outside with Sharon. She looked pumped up again. We ignored them. Tracey went up the street and I went inside my house.

Sharon called Meme. I saw Yolanda walk over so when I got in the house I kept peeking to see what was going on. They stood in a huddle talking.

Fifteen minutes later, Yolanda knocked on the door.

"Sharon told me that ya'll lil' things going around whipping ass and terrorizing shit. That's what she's been hearing. She said you just moved around here and you've got a rep already. Since she knows me and Meme, she said she wanted to meet you since you live on her block."

"So come let me introduce you."

I walked outside and waited for Yolanda to make the introductions.

"Samone, this is Sharon. Sharon this is Samone."

"I finally get to meet your bad ass huh?" Sharon said.

"Cool with me. I ain't one to go looking for no fight."

"Fine, they called me today saying Tracey had some trouble. I get up to the school and see ya'll three lil' asses. I was like, 'man stop it'. I'm not going to make my mom mad, hell no let's go. That's why I left her fat ass where she was."

"Oh really..."

"What's up with you and Tracey, Samone?" Sharon asked.

"She got caught up in feelings over Tasha."

"I heard, Nel called me last night."

"I don't feel Nel. I understand that they go way back, but she should keep her comments to herself. I'll bash that chicken-head. She just don't know who she's playing with. The next time she gets slick, I don't care where we are, I will put her in check. I'll take my chances and challenge her to a fight."

"Damn Samone, you all right with me, you smoke, girl?" Sharon asked.

"Yes I do."

"Ya'll want to hit this joint before ya'll face the music?" Sharon asked.

"That'll work." I said.

"I've got to go home." Meme said.

Yolanda and I stayed. We continued to talk with Sharon.

"I like you and Yolanda." She said. "I've watched Meme and Yolanda grow up." She said as she rolled and lit the joint.

"Yeah they told me there was this girl named Samone from Carol City over there by 183rd." Sharon said. "I had to meet you."

"Yeah, that's all right."

"You know a girl name Tangy? She's from Carol City too. She used to come up here."

"Yeah we hung out from time to time."

"She was the one who told your lil butt was feisty."

"Sharon what time is it?" Yolanda asked.

"Four-thirty," she answered.

"Really I got to go girl. Let me go clean up." I said hitting the joint one more time and racing off.

"All right Samone come over anytime neighbor and don't trip off Tracey's shit." Sharon said.

"Oh, I wasn't," I laughed.

That evening, I cooked barbequed chicken, yellow rice, with some sweet peas. By then Mamacita was home. I ate, took my bath and locked myself in my room. I knew the phone was going to ring and it all the peace would be over.

Eventually it happened. Mamacita answered the kitchen phone. I got up acting like I wanted something to drink. She tapped my shoulder as I heard her speaking.

"Your name is Walker? Seven a.m. that will be fine." She said and got of the phone. "You and your damn fighting again, Samone."

"I didn't fight." I countered.

"You were about to. The principal reported that you were cursing. I know your mouth is filthy and needs to be disinfected."

I stood quiet and listened. Mamacita only had one fight in her life. She didn't understand how mean the streets get. She called Paula and she came over and talked to me. I told her everything. She worked for a juvenile detention center and knew all about the 22nd Avenue players. She told Mamacita who called me out the room.

"Look what you got yourself into. Trouble is very easy to get in but hard to get out of."

"I'm not going to be anybody's punk or sucker."

"Ma she has to defend herself, and you can't fault her," Paula said.

"Yes…"

"You already know Samone is going to fight. You must teach her what to do in order to avoid the next confrontation."

"Yeah I guess you're right. All she has to do is keep that mouth of hers closed," Mamacita said.

The phone rang. Good now I have to get up extra early and listen to what they had to say about me. I thought as I went to answer it.

"Don't be on that phone too, too long," Mamacita said.

"Meme...Paula's here. Yeah, Mamacita called her. I'm cool. What happened to you? Ol' girl, just fuss..."

When Shellie came in the room talking about you make me sick. I knew it was time to go to sleep. The next morning Mamacita went to school with me. The principal requested to speak to the parents alone. I left and went back home. It was too early for school. Mamacita returned home and asked why I left.

"It was too early." I answered.

"You're not grown. The principal could not believe all of your mouths cursing like sailors. This is on your record. One more disruption and they'll be sending all of you to Jann Mann Opportunity," she said.

"I don't care. They keep starting shit."

"Samone, you've been suspended for five days."

"Huh...for what...?"

"The principal gave all of you fair warning and they feel this incident was gang related."

"I'm not with a gang."

"You might as well be. You and Yolanda and that Meme, she's getting transferred to Thomas Jefferson."

"What...?"

"You just need to get something in your mind before they kick you out of Dade County public schools. I want you to do all the housework, it will keep you busy."

"All right, Mamacita," I said.

"See you later," she said and was off to work.

It was a good thing that Paula was over last night. Yolanda called, then Meme called to say that she was coming out when ol' girl left for work.

"All right come around the back so that nosy neighbor won't see you." I said. We didn't have to see school for the next five days. When the girls came over, we partied and smoked, cooling out listening to music.

"You're crazy, Samone." The girls chimed as we got high.

"You be ready to fight in a heartbeat." Meme said.

"Yep, that's how it is with me. Things happen in a heart-beat. I don't feel threatened by none of these hos. Win or lose they will know that I was there."

Afrika Bambata's *Planet Rock* was in effect and the girls and I danced. Later, I cooked and we ate. Then they helped me clean-up and we napped.

"Damn what time it is?" Meme asked stirring.

"Three o'clock." Yolanda yawned.

"Shit, let's go before snitching ass, Shellie gets home," Meme said.

"Okay, are y'all coming out later?" Yolanda asked.

"I'm going to chill and see what Mamacita sez."

"Everything's clean, you cool? Plus, that shit ain't our

fault. That fat ass Tracey went and got help — not us. We were leaving school and minding our own business," Meme said.

"Let's hang out, go to clubs together, talk on the phone, get in dudes cars, smoke their weed, drink their drink, they drop us off where they found us. But don't let them take advantage." Yolanda said.

After they left, I thought about everything they said. I started thinking Jann Mann won't be so bad. Catch the bus getting away from the neighborhood if it came down to it then that was what it would be.

"Samone!"

"Huh...?"

"Where was your mind?"

It was Shellie. I must have drifted off.

"Dag, it's clean up in here and the food ready and all. You making sure you don't get in anymore trouble, huh?"

"Ma already knows she told me to cook and clean up."

"Damn you clean her room too."

"How'd you know?"

"Mamacita doesn't dust. Shoot, you should stay home more often."

"Girl, shut up".

"I heard they're going to be jamming in Over Town for Thanksgiving. So keep it up cause I know you want to go."

"Really...?"

"They ask me in school is your sister name Samone? I said why? They were like we heard about yesterday."

"Hmm, hmm..."

"I told them you ain't scared and the lil girl, started arguing and the teacher said she was going to call my mother. Shoot
they don't jump out there about my sister, and that's what I'm
going to tell Mamacita."

"Now your lil butt in trouble she's really going to trip out.
She'll probably laugh and say, that's all I need both schools calling."

I was staring out the window as I spoke to Shellie and
cringed when I saw Mamacita kiss Paula goodbye. It reminded me
of when a man kissed a woman.

Mamacita walked in.

"I'm getting more calls at work than ever, what's the story
Shellie?"

# 14

SORT OF
DIFFERENT
MATURING

By spring that year, I had managed to stay out of trouble. I started hanging with Yolanda and Meme again. We knew a lot of dudes and everywhere we went we always had a ride. Mamacita didn't mind if I was going with Meme. She looked at her as my big sister. She didn't know that we smoked, drank and went partying all the time.

One Friday night I got so drunk, Meme was scared for me to go home.

"Mamacita went out. I can beat her home."

"Get your lil ass in the house now, take a bath, brush your teeth, and I'll see you tomorrow." Meme said when we got there.

I staggered in and did just that. Then I went in the kitchen and raided the refrigerator. That was the best sleep. I woke up at two and no one was home. Shellie later came through the door carrying bags with groceries.

"Hi sleepy-head, we went to breakfast."

"Dag, ya'll didn't wake me."

"You're the one who wants to sleep all morning." Mamacita said as she walked in. "Go get some bags out the car. All you do is stay out at night and sleep all day. You're always doing the same damn shit all the time. You're not slick."

I never liked to miss out when she would take us to dinner. She did this every two weeks. We always went to Victoria Station. Red Lobster, where I ate my first frog leg. Tasted good, like chicken. I can't remember the last time we did any of that. Now they sneaked to breakfast without me.

"If you wanted to go to breakfast then get up early." She said.

It's cool, I live and learn. If she wanted me to go, I would have.

"Ma…"

"Yes…"

"What are you cooking?"

"I was thinking about spaghetti."

"Could you please fix some ah…?"

"What?"

"Black eye peas and rice with okra, fried chicken smothered in gravy, and corn bread."

"I'll think about it."

That usually means no. I never get what I ask for, but this time it happened. She got worse and I got worse. Even Shellie got tired of blackmailing me. She told Mamacita about me and the girls picking up boys at the bus stop. Mamacita grabbed the extension cord and began swinging it. I caught her hand.

"I'm too old for you to keep hitting me with extension cords."

"You out there standing at the bus stop and getting in cars with boys. Samone, don't you know what can happen?"

She tried to swing. I grabbed her hand. Then she attempted to snatch the extension cord. I wouldn't let go.

"I'm tired of you hitting me. I'm fifteen years old I won't heal up right. I don't want to be bruised forever from your abuse."

She grabbed my neck and threw my head in the chair and held me down.

"Don't play with me! Don't make me lay your lil ass out on the floor."

"Let me up." I yelled.

"You think you're bad?" She asked squeezing my neck.

"Just let me up! I'm going to my room."

She let go of my neck still fussing and following behind me. She ripped my phone out of the room and slammed my door. It felt like I had whiplash.

"I can't stand you. You make me sick." I screamed. "And you Shellie when I get you, it will be for everything old and new."

"You better shut your trap." Mamacita yelled.

"Your girlfriend could come up in here and have say-so. Shellie can steal my money and nothing gets done about it."

Later, I could hear her calling my name.

"Samone!"

"Huh."

"Are you going to eat?"

"No."

I did not want any of the food.  I just wanted to be grown so I can get the hell out of this house.

# 15

TIME FOR
CHANGE

A couple weeks later, Yolanda and Meme came over. They wanted to start a drill team, and you know I was all for it.

"You want me to show you some drills?" Yolanda asked.

"Yeah, let me put on my shoes and go out, Mamacita don't want anyone in her house."

Yolanda did the whole drill and step thing. I caught on real fast. Meme took a minute to get caught up. Everyone was outside, even Nel. All eyes were on us. They all liked it. We were looking real good.

Mamacita rolled up. She got out the car and swung at me.

"Didn't I tell you that I didn't want anybody in my house?"

"Ain't nobody in your damn house." I said ducking. She stared at me looking bewildered as I quickly made my way out of her reach.

"Where'd you think you're going? Come back here right

now Samone!"

"No, I'm sick of your shit." I said and stomped off.

"Damn, you didn't even do anything." Meme said catching up to me around the corner.

"I'm not going in, I'm staying out all night. I can't take it no matter what I do, good, bad, shit just don't make a difference."

I stayed out that night with nowhere to go. Meme and Yolanda stayed out as long as they could.

Mamacita did not come looking for me. She didn't care one way or another. With no money in my pockets, I wandered the street for a while. I couldn't go far. I went under the carport and tried to open the car door but it was locked. I sat on the car for a while then I sat on the cold ground.

Daylight came so I knocked on the door; she let me in and said she was getting ready to call the police. She probably called Paula and found out what to do.

"Are you going to school?" She asked.

"Yeah," I said and took a shower, got dressed then left back out without saying another word.

"Do you want lunch money?"

Mamacita called after me. She handed it to me and I kept going. I walked around for about two hours, came in the back way and went to sleep.

I was bitter and very distant the last months of school. I got in several arguments. The major one occurred one day with Nel and Tasha.

"I'll beat you down, Nel." I screamed as Meme and Yolanda arrived on the scene.

The principal intervened and took us all to the office.

"What is the problem?" he asked.

There were no answers.

"Does anyone want to fight? Because I'll take you to the locker room and you can go at it."

"Fine with me, I got a lot to get off my chest." I said.

"Not me," Nel and Tasha replied.

"Samone, you want to fight huh?" the principal asked.

"Yeah, I want to get it over with."

"Well, neither of them wants to and if you fight, five days and when you come back five more."

"You can't do that." I said

"Want to try me, Ms. Thang?"

She gave us passes for class. As I was about to leave she called me back.

"You are off the drill team," she said.

I was a little upset but didn't show it.

"We do not need anyone representing us with a bad attitude," she continued as I walked out of her office.

I met Yolanda and Meme when school was out. We spoke about it.

"Damn it was our shit first." They both said and both left to go practice.

That evening, I did my homework then I washed the dishes. I wasn't about to cook.

The sound of the doorbell roused me from my thoughts. I looked through the peephole it was Yolanda and Meme.

"The drill instructor was acting all funny." Yolanda started.

"Yeah we had to remind her that we were the first on this drill team." Meme interrupted.

"That new girl, Sabrina is not catching on and the parade is in two weeks."

"Who's Sabrina?" I asked.

"She's the new girl who they put to take your spot," Meme said.

"The drill instructor had the nerve to tell her that she could be just like you in front of all of us."

"It don't make me no difference," I said.

"The bitch got jazzy waving bye like she a beauty queen." Yolanda said.

"I'm through with the shit..." Meme started.

"Meme you should stay." I said interrupting her.

"Why should I? We started it together and we'll end it together." Meme said with determination.

"We look all wrong with that fat ass Sabrina, looking all nervous." Yolanda said.

"That shit sure seems like a set up," I said reflecting.

"Okay, I hear that, Samone," Meme said.

"I'm not going to get in any trouble because softball is coming up next and that's my sport. I want to play," I said.

"I heard tri-outs will start in a couple weeks," Yolanda said.

"So you're going to be good, huh Samone?" Meme asked smiling.

"Yep, I'm on my best behavior."

"Mamacita might say you can't play..." Meme started but I held my hand up.

"I'm not asking Mamacita - I'm just going to play. I can run and hit, I only stayed on for a week when I lived in Carol City because Mamacita acted shitty about that. I been playing kickball, softball, volleyball and basketball on the regular. I'm good at all sports even football, I think that's why my titties are so small. The boys used to throw that ball real hard in my chest. I caught it- made touchdowns and all." We all laughed.

"Did they tackle you?" Yolanda asked.

"Yep, they did. I never realized they were setting me up. They'd pass the ball then they all came rushing me. After doing it a few times, I caught on. My body started changing and I knew I had to stop playing football."

"You can't always do what boys do..." Yolanda said.

"Yeah, but thank God he gave us a way to beat them at their game." Meme smiled rubbing her curves.

We high-fived and laughed.

Tryouts came and of course, I made the team. Tracey found out and knew that I walked home from softball practice by myself. Yolanda and Meme were still getting in trouble. The week after I made the team Meme's mother transferred her to Thomas Jefferson.

Softball became my world. I knew Jann Mann was on the high rise. I avoided all conflicts so I wouldn't be kicked off the team. The days flew by and I yearned to play.

Friday was here, and I had a softball game. They announced it like I would've forgotten. I knew fat-ass Tracey heard it.  Mamacita was on vacation.

"I'd stay and watch but my grandmother wants me home early.  I got to do something for her." Yolanda said before leaving.

Tracey and some of her friends were watching.  While fielding, I heard one of her friends yakking away.

"Samone is good, she can hit."

"Fuck that bitch, she's gonna get her ass kicked today.  Plus it's Friday."

After the game the principal came on the field to congratulate us, the victorious Westview girls' softball team.  She spoke to the coach.

"How's Samone behaving?"

"She's my MVP," Coach replied.

"She better stay good.  One of the trouble-makers already has been transferred to Thomas Jefferson."

The principal looked around and spotted Tracey with her posse.

"You need to be on your way home, all right.  Goodbye," she said.

"Aw! Ms. Walker I'm not doing nothing."

"I didn't say you were, ladies have a good weekend."

Although we had won our first game, I didn't feel right.  I started walking and thinking.  I wound up taking the long way home.

By the time I reached near my house, I saw that there was a crowd in front of Sharon's house.

"You scared bitch?" Tracey asked.

"Fuck you fat bitch!" I said and went inside my house.

"What's going on?" Mamacita asked as soon as I walked through the door. "You're acting like you up to sump'n. Anyway I need a stick of butter for this cake I'm baking for Paula's birthday," she said.

"Those girls trying to start and I don't want to get suspended from school. I want to play on the softball team. Plus, if I have one more fight they're going to send me to Jann Mann."

"Them girls, that's all I hear. All right go to the store," she said.

Right then and there, if I never knew before, I knew she didn't give a damn about me.

The crowd watched as I walked by Sharon's house.

"Oh shoot Tracey, look she ain't scared," someone said.

When I reached 22nd Avenue, I saw Meme and Yolanda across the street.

"Walk with me to the store," I said.

As we strolled across the street, we noticed a crowd following us.

"When are you going to fight her, Tracey?" Someone asked.

"Wait until we get to the store," was the answer.

I went inside the store and picked up the butter. Then I decided to play Super Pac Man. While playing the game, Tracey came up to me.

"You wanna come outside and talk shit now, bitch?" she asked.

"Can't you see I'm playing my game?" I answered.

She pushed my head real hard. I gave the butter to Meme

and went outside.  She grabbed me before I got set.

"I'm going to make you eat my pussy," she said while try-ing to push my head down between her knees.  I almost passed out from the smell of her funk.  As the store-owner broke up the scuf-fle, I stuffed my right fist in her mouth and ran while he held her. I found an empty soda bottle and broke it.  Then I ran behind her to stab her in that fat ass neck.

"No Samone.  Don't do it," Meme said grabbing my hand.

"You bitch, you busted my lip.  Now your crazy ass, wanna stab me?" Tracey screamed.

I quickly found another bottle and broke it.

"I'll kill your big ass.  I don't give a fuck."

"You need to simmer down and come with me," Maurice said grabbing me.

He walked with Yolanda, Meme and me down the street.

"You don't play for real, huh shortie?" Maurice asked.

"All she did was grabbed me like fat bitches do.  She needs to wash that stankin' coochie!"

"She ain't gon' be messing with you anymore, Samone," Yolanda said.

"That's why I gave her that fat lip."

I had a major attitude by the time I got in the house and Mamacita was not in the mood to be sympathetic.

"I told you not to fight!" she screamed.

"They started, and what?"

"Look at your hands.  You're bleeding."

"Here's your butter, I had to fight."

"Go clean yourself up," she said.

Mamacita got evil after that. She didn't give-a damn if I stayed out all night. She would go nuts when I missed my curfew, which was often.

"Go back where you came from!" she would scream. "I don't want you corrupting my daughter. Go sleep in the car like you did before."

She totally stopped giving me any type of support.

"Let those men you sneaking into their cars with give you their money!"

She would yell at me whenever I complained. I had to do something really fast or I felt like I would lose my mind.

JANN
MANN

# 16

Monday morning came and the names from Friday's melee outside the store, were announced over the loudspeaker.

"Samone Johnson you were warned." The principal said as soon as I walked into the office.

"It was four o' clock, actually way past four," I said.

"That does not justify you attempting to stab Tracey."

"Yes...ah no but..."

The principal didn't want to hear it.

"You're suspended for five days and Monday morning you'll start Jann Mann. That goes for you also Yolanda."

"But I didn't have anything to do with it," Yolanda said looking surprised.

"It was reported that you aided and abetted Samone."

"What the fuck you did?"

"Samone, you best watch your mouth…"

"Why? What the fuck for? Westview Junior High can't do shit to me. I'm off to the races, running with the wild juveniles at Jann Mann. Fuck Westview."

I walked out and went home. Mamacita better not come with her shit. This was all her fault. I told her stupid ass. Nah, she wouldn't listen. All she was worried about was some freaking butter.

Yolanda called and told me how scared she was to go to Jann Mann. I told her to come by my house.

"They gave me five days." She said sounding sad. "They wanted all of us out; the staff said we were worse than the boys."

"Don't worry. I know a lot of people from Carol City that attend Jann Man. You straight, I'm not going to let anyone get in your business. Shit I can't wait till Monday, new school bus to pick us up and drop us off. Look at the bright side, Yolanda."

"What's that?"

"At least you know me."

"Samone, you were really serious about the softball team," Yolanda said.

"Yeah, real serious, I love my sport. If they have a team, I'm playing."

"I hope so."

"Its all Mamacita's fault. Man, I'm not going to be in the house when she gets home. I'm coming in late tonight. I don't give-a fuck if she tells me to sleep in the car. She took my phone already. She and her punishments don't matter. I'm going to get a three cent bag and chill."

"You soo crazy…"

"This weekend will be the battle of the deejays. I'm not going to part my lips and ask to go. All for some damn butter to bake Paula's cake. She could've got in her cougar and gotten her own butter. Her lazy, lazy ass self makes me sick. She better not start with me this Monday night."

"Who's that?" Yolanda asked.

"Sounds like she's here already, maybe it's Shellie," I answered.

"The way things have been going, it could be your nosey ass neighbors." Yolanda laughed.

"You could be right." I said thinking. Either way, I didn't want to around to find out. "Let's go get a bag and head over to Sharon's house." I suggested.

Maurice ran up on us.

"Y'all fittin' to cop again? Y'all be steady getting up. Where you been getting all this money from? And don't tell me y'all working or your mother be giving it up?"

Why was Maurice all up in the business? I was about to let him have it, but saw a couple standing next to him.

"You know better, we're stressed." I said with a wry smile.

"Oh, I see…these are my friends. Wanna hang?"

They were standing next to a shiny new car. It was a no-brainer that Maurice's friends had money. Me and Yolanda looked wide-eyed at each other and decided to roll. We headed to the other side of town and easily got into the club. The couple we were with knew the owner. Inside the place was a strip joint. We sat close to the stage and watched the girls stripping down to bra and panties and gyrating only to disappear and a new crew would be dancing.

As the night wore on we found out that Maurice's friend was a dancer. "An exotic dancer," she called herself. She danced loosely on the stage. After that Yolanda and I quizzed her about the life.

"Oh, you could make over two to five thousand a week."

"Wow!"

Yolanda could not contain herself. She immediately started dreaming of doing make-up and disguises.

"It pays...the car we're riding is a gift to my baby." She said kissing her man's smiling cheek.

Later we smoked a couple joints and both Yolanda and I were convinced that we could do this and make a lot of money without anyone finding out. Maurice was able to convince us that we would need protection which he could provide for a fee. The plan was brewed and Yolanda and I were ready to start the following weekend. Money was taken care of and I was about to take on Jann Man, I needed all the edge.

"It's tasteful because you dance in bra and panties." Yolanda noted.

"Yeah and it's of your choosing, but the sexier attracts more attention which equals more money."

She got back on the stage sliding up down the pole. Yolanda and I sat mesmerized as she rolled her ass. Dollars rained on her act as she popped, locked and gyrated her hips. All the men's eyes were focused on her. It was clear that her act had hyp-

# 17

The next morning Mamacita woke and made breakfast. Paula must have stayed the night.

"Well, I heard from your school. Your principal informed me that a bus will pick you up and drop you off startng Tuesday. You probably know half the school. A lot of your old cut-buddies probably are there by now."

"Yep, I guess…"

"It's nothing to smile and be happy about. It does go on your records."

"Yeah I know."

"You don't even care, do you?"

"Nope…"

"You hear that Paula? I'm not bothering her."

Paula probably told her to leave me alone, a good thing. I

knew she didn't care for me.  If Paula wasn't coaching her, I don't know what would've happened.

I slept most of the day and later, Yolanda and I discussed waiting awhile before telling Meme about our plan.

I got in the shower; I was still so high and had some serious munchies, something terrible.  I saw chicken that Mamacita had made from the night before.  I wanted to fuck the rest of that chicken up.

I was happy to eat without Mamacita staring in my face. I ate three pieces of chicken, two helpings of Cole slaw, a biscuit and some fruit punch.  It was time for bed again.  I had no privileges.  When Mamacita was home I couldn't be on the phone.  No TV.  All I could do was say my prayers and go to sleep.

"Samone, Samone."

"Huh."

"I'm gone to work.  Some chicken in there you can have for lunch all right."  I smiled.

She hadn't caught on yet, that's the ticket.  The week was almost over.  Monday morning was approaching and I was ready for the new school.  Yolanda was getting nervous.  Meme stopped by.

"Samone, I heard you're going to a new school," she said.

"That's right."  I started laughing.

"Dag, Yolanda you don't look too, too happy."

"They sending me there and I did nothing."

"Girl, get over it."  I said.

"You just don't know..."

"I know...Yeah girl, plenty boys from Carol City,

Opalocka, Over Town, Liberty City...mad variety," Meme said.

"Okay, yeah, hurry up Monday. Thanks Meme, I can't wait now."

"Monday can't get here soon enough for me. Westview didn't have any boys except for Maurice and his crew," I said. Yolanda cleared her throat.

"Oh, don't tell me you had some that?" Meme asked. Yolanda and I smiled.

"No, him and his crew were spoken for. Plus you got to give your coochie up to all of them. Westview have only junior high boys."

"Yeah, Thomas Jefferson has a few potential fellas," Meme said with a wink.

We started walking up the street.

"I can't go far, so I'll see y'all later," Yolanda said.

Meme and I walk toward Johnson Carwash. Before we knew it we were walking in to see if Kevin was there. I could entertain myself with him sweating me.

"Damn, baby you holding..." he said patting my ass. Meme smiled.

CAN'T STOP
FIGHTING

# 18

I was ready for the drama of a new school.  I started seeing people
I hadn't seen in eons.  The first week was filled with running into
people I knew from my past.  I knew I was going to look forward
to all the up coming events that Jann Mann had to offer.

That Friday was the first day of our weekend.  Yolanda
and I started our dancing routine.  We both dressed as nurses.  In
the dressing room Yolanda applied the make-up.

"You look really nice, Samone."

"May our good looks get us a lot of money," I said toasting
and swallowing whiskey.

It was good to be on stage with someone I knew.
Otherwise I don't think I could've done it.  Although I took two
more shots of whiskey before going on, I was nervous.  Sweat
poured off me from the heat of the bright lights.  My head spun

and I started to dance slowly to keep from vomiting as eyes stared at me. Then I started relaxing and moving my hips. By the end of the song we had to begin to strip.

When the third song played I felt bold and was comfortably grinding in just my panties and bra. Remembering what I'd learned the first night, mine were see-through and my nipples stuck out. I squeezed them and the men howled. They tried to grab my ass but the bouncers wouldn't let them near.

It was clear that I was their favorite. They threw wads of money at me. I kept bending down to collect money, showing my ass as I did. That night I had more money than I ever had in my entire life. It was a little over a thousand dollars.

Yolanda had three hundred and together we split our money with Maurice, who stuck around until we were finished with our routine. Then we went out drinking and smoking before going home. We repeated the process on Saturday. We wound up splitting eighteen hundred dollars between the three of us.

My second week of school, I was in orientation. I am chilling listening to the teacher when this boy barked at me.

"Move your arm one more time and I'm going to punch you right in your jaw!"

"Go ahead and do it." I hollered back.

"Put your arm up there again."

I did it. He moved it and pushed me. Then he stood up so I stood up. He swung, I ducked. He picked me up and tried to body-slam me. I pushed all my weight forward and he fell backwards with me landing on top. I sat on him and just started punching him in his face. I did not stop until the teacher broke it up.

"Both of you go to the office," he said.

The boy who I had been fighting had a knot on the side of his head.  All the fellas were laughing.

"Ah man...Samone whipped that ass," echoed through the halls as we walked to the principal's office.

"Let's tell him we made up and it won't happen again," the boy said before we walked inside.

The principal went for it.

"Because this was your first time I'm going to give you both a chance."

"Samone what's up?" I heard you were fighting?" Yolanda asked when I saw her later that day.

"Yeah..."

"And she whipped the dude's butt," someone added.

"She didn't do nothing to me."  The boy said as he walked by us.

"You want part two?" Someone quipped.

"You going to get jumped next time."

"What in the world is that coming down the hall?" I heard someone asking.

"Looks like a big Mac with glasses."  Another student observed.

Yolanda and I turned around and started laughing when we saw Tracey Smith.  I guessed they put her out.  She looked real scared when she recognized us.

"Ain't that the bitch I was fighting?"

"That's why I'm here," Yolanda said.

Three days after Tracey got there, she was running her mouth all over the school. She punched some guy in the face and he body-slammed her big ass. After that incident, Tracey became the best student in the entire school.

Yolanda was doing the weekend gig at the club and so far everything was going well. I was learning fast and realized that touching and playing with my private areas, not only turned the men on, but also turned me on.

Friday and Saturday I would dance and by Sunday I had to be locked up with Kevin, getting my coochie tore out all day. I was growing so hungry for sex that he was asking what was wrong.

School was a drag. I still had beef every now and then. One day I was holding a chair for Yolanda in the lunchroom.

"Could I have this seat?" Some boy asked.

I had my leg on the chair.

"Someone is sitting here," I said firmly.

"They aren't sitting now."

He snatched the chair from under my leg. I stood up and didn't give him a chance. I punched him in the head about three times. A teacher broke it up. All the fellas kept asking: Why did you break it up, man?

"Two more punches in the head, he would have been out, she daze him." They hollered and hooted at me.

From that day on they call me Lil' Sugar Ray. Everyone had mad respect for me.

"Samone, they're having tri-outs for softball, you down, right?" Yolanda informed me.

"You know it.  Just like old times, girl."

"I heard that you get out of classes to have practice."

"That will work very well."

I signed up.  We played a lot of good teams and won second place.  I remembered receiving the trophy.  All I ever dreamed of.  It was something I did for me.  I cherished that moment.  When they had the awards assembly, my name was called.  Samone Johnson, softball team Jann Mann Opportunity.  I felt so happy I could not wait to show Mamacita.  I didn't tell her about me playing softball.

"I didn't know that you were playing softball."  She proclaimed after I had explained the whole thing.

"Uh huh..."

"They let ya'll lil butts have a softball team?" Mamacita joked.

"Yep..."

"That's a nice trophy."  She finally beamed.

I walked away thinking that I'd go to summer school.

"Hi Samone," Shellie greeted me as she walked in.

"Hello Shellie."

"Mamacita sez she's gonna get our phone turned back on."

"Okay, are we going to have the same number?"

"Yep..."

"Good..."

"This is a nice trophy.  Too bad y'all weren't first place."

'Somebody's gotta win and somebody's got to lose..."

"Samone ...Shellie." Mamacita shouted disrupting.

"Yes..." we shouted back.

"Ya'll in the house?"

"Uh huh…" Shellie answered.

"What, are y'all sick?" Mamacita asked.

"Nope, just talking," Shellie said.

"I'm going next door, Samone are you going out?"

"In a little while," I answered.

"Yeah of course, you're never home on the weekend."

"We're gonna hang at T.Y. Park." I lied.

"Who are we?"

"Our school, for our last day of school field trip. Could you bake some bake beans?"

"I hope you didn't tell them people I was going to make baked beans."

"No…" I started and shook my head.

"What's wrong Samone?" she asked.

"Nothing really," I answered and walked away leaving Shellie watching TV. Thoughts ran wild in my head.

"Are you high?"

"No," I answered and took a deep breath then entered my room.

I was finally able to put my mind on something and made it happen. I had money. I pulled the shoebox from under the bed. I counted thinking, I could buy anything I wanted. I could be a model. I was twirling around in the room and heard the door open. Shellie walked in.

"What are you laughing at?" I asked.

"You're acting a little crazy. I thought you were smoking and… Damn Samone where you get all that money?"

"Girl, wait!" I tried to block her view but she was all over it.

"Is it real?"

Shellie put her fingers on the bills like they weren't real. She smiled wide eyed when she realized these were dead presidents.

"You can't let Mamacita know. It's Kevin's. He doesn't want anyone to know about it. We're saving to get married."

"That's good. What's up with all the one dollar bills?"

"Get out of here. He's got some fives, tens and even twenties here."

"Shoot he's got enough to buy a car. How much he's got so far?"

"It's supposed to be two thousand. You know what, let's count it together and we'll take some and go shopping tomorrow."

"No, I don't wanna mess with Kevin's money like that," Shellie said and walked out.

I had to hide my loot, I thought.

Later that night, Yolanda came by with Maurice and we left with his friends in their nice expensive car. Another Friday night and the club was packed as usual. There was a mostly Latin crowd on Fridays, so Yolanda always made us up to look Spanish. I was gonna get down tonight. I sat and sipped whiskey thinking I had enough money to buy a car. I wanted more.

On stage I was captivating as usual, throwing my legs with ease. I was Cinnamon and Yolanda, Candy. We descended on the crowd of wild Latin men rolling our hips and rotating our waistlines. Dollars rained as I emulated moves I caught from the first strip show I saw.

The place was hot and were about to close our set, when I saw them. Mamacita, Paula and Kevin were trying to get in. I saw them when they walked down to the stage area, Kevin was leading. He could not immediately identify us, but he saw Maurice and it wasn't a friendly greeting. Yolanda and I slipped off stage and ran into the dressing room. We quickly changed and grabbed our belongings.

"Damn! I left a lot of dollars on that stage," I said rushing out the backdoor.

"How did ol' girl found out?"

"I don't know but we gotta beat them home and come up with a story on the way."

We jumped into a taxicab and gave Yolanda's address. My heart was thumping so loudly in my chest I sat hugging myself. I closed my eyes. Yolanda kept looking back as if we were being chased.

"What're you gonna tell them?"

"First thing is I'm gonna find out who told Mamacita and then I'm gonna smash some heads."

"Let me know what happens," Yolanda said as she got out the cab. She handed the driver some money and I got out also.

We raced inside her house and I was about to run in her bathroom. The lights came on.

"Yolanda is that you?"

"Yes, grandma..."

"Ah...what's-her-name mother...ah came over and was asking for her. They left a message for you. I hope you're not in no kind of trouble again."

"No, grandma..."

"Well call them just in case."

"All right, grandma."

I washed and removed all traces of the make-up and hid the money with Yolanda. Then I set off to find out how our cover was blown. I opened the door and everyone was up. Kevin was staring at me. Mamacita and Paula sat together in the sofa and waited. Shellie was eating peanut butter and jelly sandwich.

"Why, Samone? Why?" Mamacita pleaded. She looked old and worn. Maybe it was her tears. Paula tried to comfort her. Kevin said nothing.

"Aren't you tired of embarrassing us?" Mamacita continued.

"Samone, now you should've known better than to cause this type of embarrassment on your mother."

"I wanna have money. I need new clothes, not hand me downs. I want to be a normal teenager and have new stuff."

"But your mother cannot afford that, she's..."

"Poor...we have nothing. I don't want to be poor like her, I'm just trying to make some money, that's all."

"But you don't have to strip for it..."

"It's erotic dancing. It's not stripping..."

"Paula you're wasting your time arguing with her. She's gonna tell you being a whore is only..."

"I ain't no fucking ho!'"

"Samone, that's your mother..."

"Let her fucking curse and be disrespectful, now everyone

can see her true colors," Mamacita said.

"True colors, embarrassment...? You should hear what they saying about you and your girlfriend Paula..."

"They call you a bull-dyke...a poor ass broken down bull-dyke."

Every once in a while we overstep our boundaries. Agreeing to dance at the club was one; calling out my mother and her lover was another. I couldn't go back. I stomped off in the direction of my room.

"Where are you going?"

"Let her be Mamacita...I'll talk to her." Kevin said.

He approached me as I stood outside my room. His clothes were torn and he had bruises on his hands. I could tell that he had been fighting. That's the reason I even let him near me, I knew he cared.

"Samone, what's up with you, girl?"

"Can't you tell I'm trying to make some dough..."

"Why'd you tell Shellie that it was my money and all that...?"

"Shellie's a nosy ass bitch. Wait until this blows over. I'm a kick her ass so badly for everything she's ever done to me."

I was sure who had blown this whole thing up. It was nosy ass Shellie. She asked Kevin and he had no idea about the cash.

"You should've let me in on it and then you could've..."

"So Shellie told you and how they found out?"

"Man, I was suspicious. I had asked Meme and she was like you might be cheating with boys from your new school that

Yolanda and you met..."

"My cousin Meme, she needs to mind her own fucking business."

"Your mother saw you leaving in an expensive car, she calls my house and I don't own no car."

"That's a fact..."

"You told me you were hanging with Yolanda. They went to Yolanda's and her grandma told them she left with Maurice. Then I checked with some of his peeps and bam we came to check you..."

"You had to bring the whole cavalry with you?"

"Don't try to make it seem like I was the one who was dancing naked for money..."

"I'm doing for me.  What can you do for me?"

"I can get a real job and work and..."

"Be poor all your life depending on hand me downs...."

"C'mon Samone you ain't got to strip like you a ho or sump'n."

"Kevin you're getting on my last fucking nerves.  You need to get da fuck outta my house before I..."

"Call your pimp Maurice.  That nigga should've checked into the hospital by now..."

He pointed his finger and took a step toward me.  I took the ice-pick from my purse.  Kevin got the point real quick and stepped.

I went in my room and saw that they had searched the hell out of it.  I headed straight to where I hid it.  The shoe box with the money was gone.  Fuck it! It was fun while it lasted.  I still had like about two hundred stashed at Yolanda's. I supposed my family would now disown me.

I stayed in my room for the rest of the weekend. Paula stayed because I didn't hear Mamacita's mouth. Shellie knocked on my door Sunday afternoon.

"Samone, you better hear what I have to say to you."

"I don't wanna talk to no snitch..."

"Samone I didn't tell on you. It was Meme. Let me in and I'll tell you what happened."

I opened the door and she walked in looking innocent.

"Okay you better not tell anymore lies..."

"Friday night when you left out with Yolanda, Mamacita said she saw the expensive car. She was asking whose car it was but I didn't know. Then she spoke to the neighbor and they told her about the pimp who owns the car. Then Kevin came and I mentioned the money and he was like I don't know about any money. Mamacita asked him about you dancing and where. Kevin started calling everyone who knew Maurice until he found out everything. Then while they went to get you, I took the money and hid it."

"So you didn't give it to Mamacita?"

"No, of course not, us sisters got to stick together."

"Where's the money?"

"It's in Mamacita's room..."

"In Mamacita's room? That's the stupidest shit I ever..."

"Calm down, big sis. She and Paula went out. Stay here I'll go get the money."

Shellie brought the shoe box with the money and the telephone.

"Yolanda's been trying to reach you," she said.

"Why you being so nice, Shellie?"

"I told you, sisters must stick together."

It was probably about the money. At least she didn't give that to Mamacita. I dialed Yolanda's number.

"It was crazy up in here, this weekend...Shellie hid the money...you wouldn't believe where...Yeah gotta hook her up, she was nice. You heard from Meme...?"

"That bitch..."

# 19

Late Sunday night, I heard the car pull-up and I went to the window to see.  Paula was driving and I didn't see Mamacita.  Paula came in alone.

Where was the ol' girl? I wondered trying to read the expression on Paula's face.

"Girls…" Paula shouted.  "Girls," she repeated as me and Shellie came running out.  Something must be up.  Maybe Mamacita got arrested for beating up someone in the mall.  "Girls your mother is in the hospital…" she blurted and ran off.

"What do you mean?" Shellie screamed running after her.

She returned with Shellie still running behind her.

"She fainted…ah maybe too much stress and you all know that your mother works real hard," she said looking at me.

"Faint…?" I repeated.  You don't go to the hospital for

fainting I was thinking.

"When is she gonna be out?" Shellie asked.

"Maybe tomorrow...I don't know.  Now tomorrow you both have school, right.  So you'll have to wake up and pretend it's a normal day, okay."

I nodded and Shellie began to cry.  I hugged her and we walked to the room together.

"She's gonna be alright.  Mamacita ain't gonna stay too long in any hospital."  I said.

Before long we were talking about how Mamacita wouldn't take us shopping for school.

"Let's go shopping tomorrow..." I started.

"Let's buy Mamacita something special."  Shellie interrupted.

Next morning we awoke.  Paula stuck around.  Me and Shellie smiled and talked.

"Remember you two should be on your best behavior." Paula said.

Shellie was all for it.  Whatever she meant sounded good to us.  We were snapping while getting dress.  I walked her out the door.  She hooked up with Nel's sister and I waited for the bus.

I didn't want to miss a day of school, always something going on.  Everyday was fun.  They made you want to do class work.

The bus showed up: Reform school for the misbehaved it should read.

Jann Mann was live five days a week.  The students snorted coke with no shame in their game.  They have it right in dollar bills and carried it on field trips. I would sit and watch as they shoved the powder up their noses. Yolanda came on the bus.

"Another day at Jann Man," she announced sitting next to me.

"Yep..." I said giving her a pound.

"I hope we get there soon, I'm hungry." I said.

"Three more stops and we're there."

When we were inside the school, I noticed the line.

"Dag, everybody bum-rushing breakfast this morning, huh?"

"Girl, you know they've got good breakfast."

"These kids are probably high." Yolanda said.

"Breakfast is good."

"Okay, they look like they have the munchies though."

"Samone, I got a joint, after breakfast, if you and Yolanda want to walk into the woods." One of the cute Miami boys said.

"All right," I smiled.

After we had eaten, we walked down to the wooded area and smoked. We were busy chatting when all of a sudden, we heard rustling. It was security coming at us.

"Look out!" the boy yelled.

All of us hauled-tail the boy took off first.

"Follow me," he said.

We broke, even faster. The boy had done it before and he knew the way to the houses.

"Samone, Bob was looking for you," a girl said.

"What I'm, a dick teaser?" I smiled at Yolanda.

"That's the way, smoke they weed then leave." The boy

said as he walked by us.

"Mamacita is in the hospital and I'm really worried." I said

"Samone you're always worrying. Here, take the money you left Friday nigh with me. That should keep your worries down."

"I'm all right, I'm glad Shellie didn't give her the rest."

"What's on the schedule?"

"We've got a movie in the morning. After lunch, we play softball, girls against the boys."

"You know I'm for it. Let's get to homeroom."

We watched Rocky 3, and after lunch it was on. You could hear all the teachers. The male teachers were cheering and letting the fellas get a little rowdy. Then Coach called for us.

"Where are Samone, Lisa, Karen, Ronda, and Darchell?"

We showed up ready the female softball team against the males. The boys were having some problems making a decision.

"We want the female team to bat first." The coach suggested.

"Nah, man let them be in the field first." A male team member shouted.

"Negro please, you know what it is." We shouted.

"Let the game begin," yelled someone.

We lost the game but they had a great cook-out after and that was a lot of fun. I forgot about Mamacita until I saw Shellie that evening.

"Mamacita isn't so well," she said sounding real concerned.

"Mamacita is a tough cookie.  She'll come out of this all right."

"I don't know, I tried to see her but they wouldn't let me."

"That's cause you're too young and you got to go with an adult."

"Let's go visit her, Samone."

"Okay..."

"But let's go get her some gifts to cheer her up."

I took Shellie shopping and we met Yolanda at the mall.

"I'm really sorry to hear about Mamacita.  I guess you won't be going anywhere this weekend."

"Girl, Friday, last day of school cookout.  It'll be fun, fun, fun."

Through it all we managed to buy Mamacita a robe, bed slippers and several nightgowns.  She was in good spirits when she saw us.  We gave her the gifts and she was overcome with emotion.

"Oh my, all these are for me? I must get sick more often." She exclaimed looking at the items.

"You don't have to, Mamacita."  I said.

"So when are you leaving this dreary place?" Shellie asked.

"As soon as they let me out," Mamacita said.

"Oh you should stay and rest..." I started but she cut me off.

"Ain't nothing wrong, just a little tired from all the running you've been putting me through..."

I was shocked that this woman was starting with me from

her hospital bed. I had to get up outta Dodge before her release. I was planning on running away from home as Paula walked in. She brought flowers and fruits. Her presence made Mamacita change her tone, all of sudden she became all nice and shit.

"Hey look who's here, Paula. Wow and you brought my favorite flowers..."

They got so excited they didn't see me motion to Shellie.

"I'm gonna leave, are you coming?"

"Where you going?"

"Home to pack, I'm leaving like never coming back." I said and walked away.

Friday morning came. It would be the first time that I had a weekend free. There wasn't much to do later, I wasn't dancing anymore. That was wearing me out and was getting lame anyway. Plus, Mamacita already told the manager I was underage. I'm sure he wouldn't let me in after she threatened to call the police if I ever set foot in his club. The phone rang.

"Good morning, Samone..."

"Good morning, Yolanda. Are you ready for the Jann Mann festivities?"

"Yes love, I can't wait." All right, see you on the bus. Dag, school has been a lot of fun." I said hanging up the phone.

"You like it at Jann Mann?" Shellie asked.

"Sure do. You look real fly in your outfit."

"Thanks Samone, you look really cute in yours too."

"Cute? How about fantastic...?"

"That's for the boys to tell."

"Are gonna go see ma today?"

"She's coming home today," Shellie said as we walked outside. She was off to school and thought of making my escape from home before Mamacita's return. I got on the bus and even the driver couldn't resist looking. All the boys complimented me and the girls stared jealously.

"Oh you're wearing that outfit girl," Yolanda said when she came aboard.

"I sure is." I laughed. "You should a seen the bus driver's face when I came up them steps. His jaw dropped to the floor."

"It looks like all the boys are coming to school huh?"

"Who do you think want to miss this? Would you?"

"No." Yolanda looked around in the crowded bus and smiled.

"Stop asking dumb question so early in the morning."

"Samone..."

"Huh...?"

"Here I brought you some juice," Yolanda said.

"Thank you."

"Man I can't wait to eat we are having everything watermelon, sweet potato pie, home made ice cream, all the good food ribs, chicken."

"All-right you making me hungry girl."

By the time we arrived at the park, the hamburgers and hot dogs were on. The music was playing, volleyball nets, bats and balls were all set for us. Some ran immediately for that. I went with the half trying to find a secluded spot to smoke. This girl, Lisa looked at me and winked her eye. I kept walking with Yolanda.

Guys were hollering at me.

"Come with us and let them love birds be."

We went and smoked. It was some stay stuck-weed. We sat there, all of us and didn't utter a word. Ten minutes turned into an eternity when Lisa snapped out of it.

"What the hell you have us smoking?" she asked the boy.

"My brother gave it to me, sez it was something for the soul." The boy replied.

"Well, he didn't lie. I'm going to go play volleyball." Lisa and the boy left.

"I like your hair. It looks nice." The boy complimented walking away.

"Yeah...yeah, I think I want to play volleyball." I smiled.

"Come on Samone, you're not going to spend any time with me?" Yolanda asked.

"Yeah, but I want to play volleyball."

We ate, danced and smoked some more. The last day of school was awesome. We found out that Parkway Jr. High was having a dance tonight and Bob, the boy I was smoking with, wanted me to go.

"I'll ask the old girl, if I could go. I'll let you know by seven." I told Yolanda.

"Damn Bob!"

"What's up with his girl?"

"Who cares?"

Feigning I wasn't feeling well. I stayed in bed when Shellie and Paula left to get Mamacita. I left for the party with Yolanda before they came back from the hospital.

The party was in full effect. All the boys were getting there groove on with me. Bob was feeling me. He kept glancing my way or standing too close.

"Are you going to give me some breathing room?"

"All right, I'll be right here, Samone."

It seemed like every boy wanted to dance with me. I was feeling Bob.

"Your haircut looks nice, Bob." I said when I had a chance to dance with Bob.

GOING AWAY
FROM MIAMI **20**

The summer came and I was dreaming parties.  I attended too many dances and splashdowns to count.  Most of all, Summer school was great.

"Regina's party tomorrow night."  I said to Yolanda as we sat in my room.  "I hope Mamacita don't come get me at twelve like she did the last one.  All the fellas were yelling somebody's mama is coming to get them time to go home.  I looked up, I couldn't believe it.  I was too through."

"No, she didn't," Yolanda laughed.

"Yes she did, calling my name out while I was getting my rap on.  She could've called.  I'm so sick of that lady.  Shellie can still get my money, I don't know about Mamacita."

"You still got plenty right?"

"Yeah girl, but I'm getting too grown and she tries to put

a tight rope on me."

"Samone, Regina's mother is on the phone."

"Tell her I'm coming Shellie. What could she want?"

"She probably wants you to help clean," Yolanda said.

"Yeah, Regina's birthday party is tonight."

"What time Regina's party start?"

"I don't know, but I know Shellie and Regina's lil sister can't wait, that's all Shellie was talking about."

I answered the phone and found out that Shellie was already next door at Regina's party. They were calling to find out if I was coming over.

"Dag, they act like they never been to a party before. I see you having your own party playing your music, drinking your Hennessy." I said. Mamacita walked by with glasses in her hand.

"Yep...Ya'll party next door I party by myself." She said.

"You should go out." I smiled.

"You know I don't go nowhere too much I'll just enjoy myself right at home. You're the party animal. You party enough for all of us."

"Right!"

"Are you about to get in the tub?"

"Yep...I was."

"Let me get in there before you get in the tub." She smiled.

"Mamacita is all right sometimes," I said to Yolanda.

"That's a cool thing..."

"Yeah, we get along fine. Sometimes we even have peace. Of course when she wants to, she makes me mad. That's when that bitch turns into a mannish motherfucker.

"She sure can flip…"

"You know it can happen in a minute with her!"

"Samone, I'm out the bathroom."

One of my favorite The Stylistics was playing on the radio. I was snapping, clapping and singing.

*You're a big girl, now…*

*No more daddy's little girl, anymore…*

Mamacita started singing. I went into the bathroom feeling happy. Then I got dressed and Yolanda and I walked next door. Everyone greeted me.

"Hi Samone…"

"Hello everyone," I answered.

I walk in the backroom. Who did I see? Shellie and everyone sitting around her, and all I see is colors, the Miami Dolphins colors, and boys feeling on her.

"Shellie", I said walking up to her. "What are you doing?"

"It's cool."

"I don't give a damn."

"You're not my mother," Shellie said.

"I'm going to ask you nicely to leave and I am not playing." She sat looking stuck-on-stupid. I smacked that girl so hard that Regina's mother came over.

"What was that noise?"

Everybody remained quiet. The question came again.

"Samone hit me."

"Samone? What's wrong?"

"She knows."

Shellie got up crying.

"I'm going to tell."

"Samone, you should've pulled her aside."

"I asked her nicely."

"Samone your mother just called. She wants you to come home." Regina said.

"Man, she's starting sump'n."

"She said you could come back". Regina said as I was walking out.

"Shellie just got to try and aggravate me some kind of way. I better not get a beaten for this." I said as I walked inside. Mamacita was standing there looking a little bent.

"Why did you slap her?"

"She knows…"

"Because of this, you're not going out next week…"

"You already said…"

"I didn't say you could…"

"You said if I have my own money."

"You don't slap her. I told you about putting your hands on her."

"Yeah, all-right, it's an outrage. I'm gone."

"Don't you go out this house, Samone. If you do, leave my keys."

"Take your damn keys." I said and she grabbed me. Shellie laughed.

"Get off me!" I yelled and snatched the knife off the table. I thought about it for a moment and put it down.

"I don't need a knife for you. I'm sick of you two mother-fuckas and this evil-ass house. Ever since we move here, shit ain't been right," I said and tried to walk out the door. Mamacita pushed me up against the stereo. I went into the bathroom.

"She's been smoking weed in there, Mamacita." Shellie said.

"You mother-fucking right I smoke. Every fucking day I have to smoke to come up in this mother fucker and deal with ya'll shit."

Mamacita shook her head in disbelief.

"Don't you walk out that door..."

"You've put me out before..."

She grabbed me and I grabbed her back. I slung her in the chair, jumped on her and put her in a headlock. I started punching her in the forehead. Shellie came charging at me. I kicked her in the stomach so hard she tumbled silently backwards.

"Go get help Shellie," Mamacita yelled. Shellie was too busy holding her stomach and crying to do anything else.

"Are you going to leave me alone?" I yelled putting my lock tighter.

I had completely snapped. I didn't want to let up even though I heard her pleading.

"Samone, I'm sorry please..."

Regina's mother and Yolanda came from across the street, by this time.

"Samone get off your mama, girl."

I let up and they helped Mamacita up.

"Are you all right?" they asked.

"I don't want her in my house." She said pointing at me.

She was old and out of breath. When her breathing

returned to normal, she was able to speak again.

"Get your stuff and go."

"You can't just put her out like that." Meme's mother said.

"She's put me out before, telling me to go sleep in the car."

"Samone, you shouldn't talk to your mother like that."

"I'm calling her daddy. She can go live with him."

"Good, I 'm tired of living here any way."

"It ain't that difficult," she said as she walked to the phone.

In a few minutes, I had packed my things and went next door.

"What happened?" Everyone was curious.

"They were over there fighting," Regina's mother said.

"Oh Samone's mama was beating her?"

"No! She was whipping the momma ass."

They all just looked at me. No one said a word. That night I asked God to forgive me. From that night on I knew that it would be best for me to talk my problems out instead of letting them build up.

The next night Regina, Yolanda and I went to the splash down. I partied and tried to forget everything. Sunday morning I was chilling when the phone rang. Mamacita called to speak to me.

"Samone you need to come home." Paula said. Mamacita probably put Paula up to this.

"How long did you think you were going to stay over there before you wore your welcome out?"

"We just got back from the splash down."

"Your mother sez she didn't give you permission to go."

"Tell her, I paid my way.  I have money."

"She wants you to know that your flight leaves at three pm next Saturday."

"Good!" I said and went home.  I started packing my suitcase then went to the kitchen to fix a plate.

"Did you ask me if you could have some of my food?"

"No..."

"Well, could I at least have some of your juice?"

I drank a glass real fast then took the second one to my room.  I was on the phone, when she invaded my privacy.

"Give me that phone." She snatched it. She was still trying to pick a fight.

"May I take a bath please?"

"Yeah..."

I took a bath and went to sleep.  Monday was here I had nothing to say to Shellie.  I just wanted Saturday to get here real fast.  Mamacita allowed me and Yolanda to go to the mall.  I told her what was going down.  Yolanda was sad to know I would be leaving but man, we had fun.  We shopped I bought underwear, bras, stockings, few pair of socks some outfits, shoes.  I spent the money in wild abandon, easy come easy go.  We laughed away the next couple days.

Saturday came and I was boarding the plane to D.C.  Now I can be with my daddy.  I still had money and I'll be able to shop. He won't sweat me.  I kissed Shellie, Paula, and Yolanda. Mamacita had said her goodbye at home.  She never made the trip to the airport.

Leaving from Miami and going to Washington, should be a learning process. I had no plans and no clue. All I knew was that I would be living with my daddy. I would get everything I wanted. I closed my eyes dreaming of big things. I awoke to hear that in five minutes, the plane would be landing. This would be a new beginning. The past was the past. I prayed for forgiveness.

CHANGES... **21**

"Hi daddy..." I smiled when I saw his handsome dark face.

"Hi baby. This is all you?"

"No. I have some more suitcases. I went shopping."

"You did?"

"Yep, because I knew I was coming to live with you. I want to go to a new school in new clothes. You know start over fresh..."

"You don't say..." Daddy quipped and kept looking out the car window. The ride to his place was silent. The apartment building was just like I remembered. It had beautiful lobby steps on each side and that old fashion elevator. Once we got upstairs to the third floor, I could see that daddy had company. There were few female friends of daddy's sitting around drinking. Daddy led me straight to the back and into the room. He showed me where

I could put my clothes. All the females came back and said hello.

"She's cute Earl." They all agreed.

"Thank you." I said.

Daddy and his friends left out the room. He later returned.

"Do you want one of these?" he asked.

I could not believe it. Right before my very eyes was a joint. I guess the look on my face made him laugh.

"I know you smoke. I'm not going to tell you not to smoke, because you're going to do it anyway. But what I'll tell you is; smoke in the house not in public, okay?"

"Okay."

"Now do you want this?"

"No."

"You a little shy, huh?"

He laughed, gave me a hug and said: "You will be all right. It will take both of us some time. It's a little new for both of us. I'll be back. Do you want something while I'm out?"

"No."

"If you want to call your mother and let her know you made it. you can use the phone whenever you wish."

"No..."

"I'm sure you want to call your friends."

"Yeah..." I smiled.

"Alright, go ahead and do that. I'll see you later," he said and left with his friends.

The first person I called was Yolanda and told her that I could smoke.

"Okay looks like you're gonna get along with your daddy. I'm glad for you, your old girl, was always tripping on you."

"Right girl, the zoo is right around the corner and Mickey D's is up the street."

"So where is your daddy?"

"He left with his friends.  He will be back later."

"What's that noise?"

"I'm walking around being noisy, looking for that bowl, I saw the last time I was here.  Daddy left the joint on the table but that crystal bowl is not around.  Well, Yolanda I'm not going to stay on the phone long.  He don't trip but I know I'll be calling you again."

Daddy was taking too long coming back.  There was nothing left for me to do.  I smoked the joint.  Moments later the phone began ringing off the hook.  At first I tried ignoring it then couldn't.

"Hello."

"May, may I speak to Black?" a voice gruffly requested.

"Black? I think you've got the wrong number."

He verified the number.

"Yes...that's the number you're calling but..."

"Oh, you must be Breezie's... ah I mean Earl's daughter?"

"Yes...but Black isn't there."

"Okay, I'm going to try to catch them.  All right baby."

I smoked the joint, watched TV and fell asleep.  I awoke hours later, it was about ten thirty, no daddy.  His apartment was next to the elevator, I could hear when someone was getting off on this floor.  I also noticed that the TV would mess up.  Then I heard keys in the door and a bunch of female's voices.  I pretended to be sleep and I heard a voice say I'll meet her in the morning.

SHORT
BUT SWEET

# 22

I realized early that daddy kept a lot of female friends. They all slept on a mattress in the living room with him. There was a sofa but that should have been thrown out. Sometimes they would be in the kitchen for hours at a time. I didn't know Black but his name was often called. Everyone acted like he was God or something. I didn't like him even though I didn't know him. I had gotten enough messages for him already.

"Hello. Is Black there?" It was Bernice she had called at least six times already.

"No, tell him to please call Bernice, yes I'm important. I'm his ex-wife.

"Who in the hell is this Black?"

Finally one day he called.

"You are an important man," I said. "Many people call

you. I just started writing your messages down."

"Thank you I'll be there to meet you today I'm going to have to hire you for my little secretary. I'll pay you for your troubles. I'll be there in a hour or so."

I heard the elevator then someone was sticking their keys in the door. I stayed in the room because I thought it was daddy. But before my eyes a medium height, dark skinned man appeared.

"Samone...?"

"Yes..."

"Hi remember me? I'm Black. You grown into a fine lil' thing," he said extending his hand. I remembered him better now.

"Oh my gosh, now I remember we went to Grandma in Va."

"You remembered. All right." He said and went into his jean jacket pocket.

Uncle Black pulled out a stack of money with a rubber band wrapped around it. "How much I owe you?" He asked giving me two fifties. "Will that do?"

"Yes!"

Since messing with Maurice and his pimp friend I've never seen anyone walking around with a stack of cash on them like that. No wonder everyone was looking for Uncle Black, he had money and a lot of it.

"From now on, Samone you'll be my secretary. If Bernie calls, tell her I'll call her after I get over my madness."

"Yeah, I think she called about a dozen times already. She's rude."

"She called being rude to you?"

"Yeah…"

"All right, wait till I see that bitch. Excuse me Samone."

I started laughing after he went into the kitchen. I went back to the room. Uncle Black stayed in the kitchen for a long time. Another set of keys open the door. This time it was daddy.

"What's up man? You met Samone?"

"Yeah she's a nice and real cute. I paid her for the phone calls that she wrote down."

"That's right up her alley. She loves money." My dad laughed then he came back to the room.

"Hi baby," he greeted walking in.

"Hi daddy," I replied with a smile.

"Do you want to go down Virginia next weekend and see your grandmother?"

"I don't care."

Daddy went back in the kitchen with Uncle Black they stayed in the kitchen for a little while longer. They both left a little later.

I was left alone on the phone with Yolanda. We spoke briefly then I heard the doorbell. Daddy didn't get home from work after midnight. I got off the phone and went to check who was at the door. It was Bernice.

"Nobody's here 'cept me." I shouted at the intercom.

"I need to see Black or Breezie. I could wait."

"Well…I ah don't know what to tell you."

"I'm on my way up…"

Few minutes later, there was knocking on the door.

"Who…?"

"It's me Bernie..."

"I told you..." I started but she knocked louder. I opened the door to see a very well dressed woman.

"I'm Bernice Johnson, I was married to your Uncle Black and I've got to see him. You have nothing to do with this but he has to come to court and they cannot find him."

"Why does he have to go to court?"

"My daughter is alleging that he sexually molested her and...Oh really this is no business of yours but I just want to see him to confront on the issue and he will not see me."

"Could I get you some water?" I asked. She nodded and I walked away.

I went to the kitchen. I couldn't face her. The same thing had happened to me. I was sexually molested and Uncle Black was the last face I remember seeing. But it could have been anyone. There were many faces at the party and it was in this same apartment three summers ago. I brought the glass with water back to her and my nerves were on edge.

She sat and drank. I turned the television on to distract my attention. I didn't want to hear anymore. Then she spoke.

"I heard you were once pregnant, is that true?"

Bad news traveled fast. She was awaiting an answer but none came from me.

"How...what did you say?" I offered hoping my stare would keep her out of other people's business.

"I mean you were twelve years old when you got pregnant. That is the same age of my daughter. Black is not her natural father, but she lived with us after we got married. Now this and he won't talk to me or the lawyers and child welfare wants to keep my only child from me. They claim that I'm an unfit mother. I love my daughter and will do anything to get her back."

She drank the water and stared at me. I pretended to be watching TV but heard every word she had said. I didn't want to think about it, my mind kept replaying that night.

We sat in the living room, me unable to face my fear and she willing to do anything for her daughter, waiting for an outcome. After a while she got up to leave and gave me a card. I closed the door and couldn't shut the thoughts out.

When daddy came I had almost forgotten about the episode until he saw the card and asked me about it.

"Bernice left it here. She thought she could find Uncle Black."

"She came here? Samone, that woman's crazy. She knows she shouldn't come here. She knows what the court papers say. Don't let her up in here. And if she comes back let her know you know about the court papers. The orders of protection sez she is to stay at least five hundred yards from anywhere Black is, she knows that."

"I didn't know..."

"It's not your fault sweetheart. She just took advantage of you that's all. That woman is vindictive and she'll do anything to ruin Black. Now she's using her daughter."

"I won't let her back up here. She walked in when the door was opened, cause I never buzzed her into the building."

"She was trying sump'n, but I'll let Black know. Don't worry about it."

Daddy left with couple of his female friends and I was alone with my thoughts again.

The week dragged by and by the weekend I was ready for my trip to Portsmouth, Va. Saturday morning we were off to see Grandma. I hadn't seen her in four years. The drive was long and slept most of the way. When we pull up to Ida Barbour, my Aunt Dottiea was at the door. She came out and gave daddy a big hug.

"Is that Samone? She got so big."

Hey kids, remember your cousin Samone.

"Samone, I have a lil girl, now." My cousin said.

"For real…?"

"She'll be home later. She's visiting with her grandmother."

Daddy and Dottiea left me talking to one of my cousins. He called my aunt and started this big family greeting thing going.

"Girl, when you got here?"

It seemed that was the question everyone wanted answered. I didn't feel like it but I obliged.

"A few minutes ago…"

"Where's your daddy?"

"Him and Aunt Dottiea went somewhere."

"I got a little girl…"

"You do?"

"Yeah…"

I found out that all the cousins I had met four years ago, were either pregnant or had a baby. This was contagious. If mine wasn't aborted I would've told the same story.

"What's her name?"

"Tanekia..."

"Okay, I'm going to walk over across the track to Swanson Homes."

Once I got across the railroad track, I walk up the street. I saw Aunt Lane she was standing outside.

"Samone..."

I ran to her and she gave me a big hug. We were going in then I heard a voice.

"Lane is that Earl's daughter, Samone?"

"Sure is..."

"Come here and give me a hug."

We hugged then she called more cousins. Everyone remembered that I was eleven the last time I was here.

"What's up stick girl?"

Carlethia came to the door. She had her baby just five days ago.

"Ya'll out here chatting I knew it shouldn't have taken that long for Samone to get here." She said.

I ran across the street and gave her a big hug. She was my favorite cousin and Aunt Lane, my favorite aunt.

"I remember him."

"How you know him?"

"The dance they had out here that summer and they were playing dice and the police chase them. He was the one who jumped over the fence. I remember his face from that day." Everyone broke down laughing.

"Oh yeah, I forgot all about that. She's right. I did jump

the fence." CB said and they all laughed again.

"Where's your daddy?"

"Him and Aunt Dottiea went somewhere."

There was a knock at the door.

"Anybody home...?"

"Earl is that you?"

Everybody went downstairs. I stayed and watched the baby sleeping. Precious little thing, I wanted to hold her but she just had a bath and ate before I got there, so I had to wait. I wanted to stay until she was up.

"Carlethia you're a mother now." Daddy said he came upstairs and looked at the baby. "You remember when you were that small?"

"No..."

He started laughing.

"Samone would you like to live here?" Dottiea asked.

"If my daddy says that I can."

The week went by real quick. Friday night they had a dance at the center. Me and my cousins went in.

*"Eat me... lick me ...I am your lollipop..."*

The deejay sang lustily.

One of my cousins began doing this wild dance, called the hawk. Different but I had fun. Daddy returned on the following Saturday and took me shopping. When we got back to my Grandmother house my Aunt Dottiea was there.

"Samone, do you want to go to school here?"

"I don't know..."

"You could go to school here if you want to?"

"Ask my daddy when he comes back.  I'm going over Carleitha's house to see the baby."

"All right I'll tell your daddy."

The whole week I got up early, Swanson Homes was on my mind.  I tried hard to be helpful thinking that daddy would say yes I could stay.  At least I'll be around family and away from that crazy Bernice woman.

# 23

MORE
SHOTS

Daddy had given the word, I could stay. My aunt registered me for school. We walked to Woodrow Wilson Senior High. My wardrobe was more than ready. I had suits, jeans, dresses, more than one pair of shoes plus Mamacita bought me a few extras. My first week of school was great. As time passed I was called to the office.

"We received your records from Florida and there was no shot record." The principal said.

"Call my house," I said.

When I came home from school, Aunt Dottiea was there.

"Samone you got to go to the clinic. I made you an appointment."

I could not believe that I had no immunization record. I had to get three in one day plus take oral medications. My arm was sore. To make matters worse, I had to come back in three months.

It sure doesn't take family long to know what's going on. My grandma babied me.

"Oh sweetie, are you alright?"

The phone rang. It was another one of my cousins calling to see if I was okay.

Later that evening my cousin came by and gave a message.

"Call your mom. She called earlier."

I had not spoken to Mamacita since I left. I didn't miss her. I was having fun and enjoying family.

"Hello..." Mamacita answered when I dialed.

"Hey Mamacita..."

We were cordial with one another and mostly talked about what I was doing and where I was currently living. I told her I was having a good time. She told me she had to go back to the hospital to get tests done and stay overnight. The doctors didn't know if she needed surgery yet.

I was sitting thinking about Mamacita and Shellie when my cousin walked in.

"You want to smoke a joint?"

"Yeah, I haven't smoked since I've been here." We lit up on the back porch. That weed had me sleeping like a baby.

Hump day, when I got to the bus stop all the students were talking about this dance-off, the Cameo Stompers battling the Play Boys. I was unaware that my cousins were dancers and in different groups, so the family was divided. Later that evening I watched and realized that my male cousins were all talented dancers.

"Samone, do you know how to roll?" another cousin asked as we headed back.

"Sure do."

"Good, we smoke but we don't know how to roll."

This was the first time that I smoked weed and drank Thunderbird in public without a paper bag.

# 24

"Samone..." It was my male cousin.

"Yeah, what you want?"

"Come downstairs for a minute."

"Uh huh..."

"You want to smoke a joint?"

"Ah...oh alright," I yawned and said.

Ever since finding out that I smoke all my cousins been hooking me up.  This one was much older and worked at the church.  He seemed like he was also drinking.

"You are fine."  He said smiling.

I was wearing only shorts and a small top without bra. His lecherous gaze made me uncomfortable.

"Let me go put some clothes on.  I didn't know it was this chilly out here."

"You don't have to. Here take my shirt," he said giving me his shirt.

We smoked and drank downstairs. There was nothing else to do. I missed Meme and Yolanda. We used to hang out all the time.

"I miss Miami," I said.

"That's right, you a Miami girl. I know you know how to do all them dances they got down there."

"Hell yeah, we have the Donkey Kong..."

"How do you do that?"

I started showing him and a look came over him. He started salivating and I stopped when he moved toward me.

"Easy, you can look but don't touch." I said with my hand raised.

"Samone, you don't have to get like that, you know? We cousins, girl," he said.

"That's why you shouldn't be all up on me like this."

"You sure are fine ass, girl." He said licking the joint.

"Fine now let me take myself upstairs."

"Samone, come back and hit the joint."

I turned around and looked at him.

"Are you coming?"

"Yeah, but don't try anything."

"You got my word."

After I hit the joint I was ready to go back to sleep.

"See Samone that's why I don't like smoking with you. You go right and lay down."

"Yep, it's twelve. I gotta get sleep."

"Grandma won't be home until about two and I'll be gone by then."

"Huh...?"

"You know you wanna give me some o' that ass."

"No way! You're craa-zee."

He was big and tried to step to me.

"Leave me alone," I said.

Then it happened right there on Vicki's porch. He began pulling me and pushing me, ripping my top. I kicked him in the groin. That only made him mad. He forced me to the floor and used his knees to pry my legs apart. I reached for the empty Thunderbird bottle and almost cracked his skull open. He was writhing in pain when I ran upstairs and locked the door.

The next day, he tried to apologize. I walked away but I could see the mark the bottle had left. I should've stuck it right to his eye. I went to school and tried to forget it.

By the time I got home, everyone knew we had the fight. Here I was far removed from Miami and my reputation was coming back to haunt me. Everyone was treating me different. After six months of living in p-town I found my self still fighting and having conversations about who they would like to see me fight.

"You could have put his eye out with that bottle you cut him underneath his eye," Aunt Dottiea said.

"So what he should not have been pulling on me."

"That's family..."

"I didn't start it, Auntie. He did."

"Go on upstairs to your room and don't come back out." She yelled and all my cousins looked at me as if I had done something wrong.

He never told how he came on to me and tried to rape me. I should be filing charges against him. Instead I was getting scorned by the family.

I stayed in the room thinking how much I missed going out to dinner with Mamacita and Shellie. Yolanda, Meme and I were always going to the movies. We used to go skating. There weren't dances anymore, only drinking, smoking and going to school. The nerve of her, we weren't seeing eye to eye. She had something to say about everything I did. If I went shopping, I had to be shopping to be impressing somebody.

It turned out that my cousin who tried to rape me, Yule, had a girlfriend and she had once filed sex assault against him.

The whole situation and the popularity of my cousins in the school had everyone laughing at me calling me of all things 'virgin'.

After that it was no more love, my aunt began to watch me like a hawk. She actually told grandma that I came in drunk and threw up all night. She never told anyone that she introduced me to heroin and cocaine. Thank God, I didn't understand the high and never really got hooked. I tried both. Once the dope drained, I felt nothing. Cocaine made my mouth numb. One day I came home from school and Auntie's buddy came over and was always flirting. I cursed his cross-eyed ass out. He went and told my grandmother that I was disrespectful.

"She said who?"

"Ms. Grown-ass in there," Aunt Dottiea said backing up his story.

"I ain't grown," I said.

"I'll come smack the shit out of you," she said.

"Come slap me," I dared.

She walked out taking off her earrings and the fight was on.  We wrestled and fell on top of my grandmother.  We were throwing down.  After a while they broke it up.

"Don't you put your damn hands on me.  You ain't my mother or father."  I yelled then I walked out.

"Samone, you get back in here."  My grandmother shouted at me.

"No I'm going over my Aunt Lane house.  She wouldn't put her hands on me because of a man."

When I got Aunt Lane's the news had spread through the entire family.  I was an outcast and misunderstood.

"What's wrong with you Samone?"

"Aunt Dottiea slapped me."

"For what?"

"Cause her friend sez I'm to grown.  He's always flirting."

"Yep, mama he always saying what he wanted to do with Samone's ass."  One of my cousins said.  Not all the family was against me.

"Yep, Dottiea was wrong," my aunt said as the telephone rang.

"Hey, yeah she's here, and Dottiea was wrong for slapping her.  The kids overheard him saying what he'd like to do for her. I'm going to call her daddy and let him know what happen. Dottiea don't make any sense."  Aunt Lane said.

"When I go back, I'll apologize for fighting in grandma's

house." I said. I went back home and aunt Dottiea wasn't there.

"Samone..."

"Yes..."

"Is that you?"

"Yes..."

"Are you okay?"

"I'm fine."

"Your daddy called, he'll call you back."

"Okay, thanks."

I sat back and thought about everything. The boys got away with everything. They had girlfriends and in this family they dominated their woman. Often they'd beat them. Grandma sided with the men and got mad when I treated myself to anything. I had to remind her that the money was mine to do with whatever I wanted. Maybe if I was a boy she would allow me to do whatever the hell I wanted.

The phone began ringing again.

"Hello, hi daddy," I answered. "Yeah, daddy she slapped me for nothing. I know, I had to defend myself. Okay, love you, daddy."

Thank God. He had heard my cry.

Too many fishes were in here. I wanted to leave because they were really fussing. Grandma, my aunts and cousins were all at it. Someone compared me to my aunt and said how I would wound up just laying around, depending on the system, or live with my momma and selling her food stamps. Then they started saying that all I did was eat all their food. What food?

It was easy to tell when the end of the month was near and

my aunt was about to re-up on food stamps. It would be pork chops one night, spaghetti the next night, followed by tuna fish, finally applesauce. She would re-up after that.

It wasn't making any difference in my life. She actually thought she was doing something. It was grandma who was reaping the benefits. It's all good that was how we were living. Fighting for food? I didn't come from that. One thing about Mamacita, she was too proud for food stamps. She felt everyone should go out and put in a day's work for a days pay. She wanted to pay her taxes and not think that other people sitting at home were living off her hard earned wages

I still had some of money left, so I went shopping. I bought me a nice pair of suede shoes from Burdines. When I got back my grandma called me.

"Samone…"

"Huh?"

"You're to clean that tub?"

"I'm about to."

I was still very upset with Aunt Dottea for slapping me. It was her man trying to get nasty with me. I guess that was how they treated men. Especially a drug-dealer and she needed her drugs. I would've been wrong if I told grandma how all these niggas be in her place when she wasn't home. I was around all these dope dealers and some of them were fine. My lifestyle was changing me. I wanted money and that hunger that made me do exotic-dance was developing.

I would hear all the moaning and groaning going on when grandma was at church and it made started to yearn for a man's touch. I couldn't remember the last time I had some. Kevin was on my mind.

I remember when I first took off my panties and opened my legs for Kevin. He was so nervous that he couldn't get it in. My cousin, Yul thought he was going to fight me and take it but no one was going to just rape me. It dragged my memory back to waking up in pain between my legs. It brought back a horrible event when I first went and stayed with daddy. I swore that that ugly situation would never happen to me again against my will.

I remembered this guy, I was horny and was gonna give him some outside in the bushes but when he pulled out that horse dick, I changed my mind. Boys are crazy they want to take you and have their girlfriends fight you.

SWEET
SIXTEEN

# 25

"Happy birthday, Samone," my grandmother greeted me as I walked in.  I had just returned from doing my favorite thing, another shopping spree.

"Thank you grandma," I said strolling past all and heading up the stairs.

I was happy my father and Mamacita had sent money.  So I had fresh outfits, shoes and money, no problem.

"You better save some of that money and not spend it all shopping for clothes."

I wanted to tell her I wasn't asking her for anything. Instead I thought about it before I really cross that thin line.

"I'll budget myself and always be prepared for the unexpected."  I smiled.

I walked upstairs thinking that I never went hungry in

Mamacita's house. Even though Mamacita was selfish and stingy, shit wasn't this bad.

I began eating out. No one should be clocking me if I wanted seconds. That's was never a problem in Mamacita house. Big pots were always on the stove and anybody who came over could eat, unless of course she was in one of her moods.

"Happy birthday Samone," my cousin Keith said.

"Happy birthday, Samone," aunt Dottiea said.

I bought a cake and we all ate slices. Grandma was in a foul mood, but I was not going to let her spoil my day. I heard when she started on last night.

"What did you do, Keith?"

"Nothing, she just started fussing."

"I see why you stay out until she's sleep."

My grades were terrible. All I did was hang-out and smoke. I did homework when I felt like. I became a C and D student, with F's thrown in. My excuse to the counselors was back in Miami it was a nine-week semester and only six weeks in Virginia. I had to get used to it. I'd promise to do better.

Smoking and drinking, I was partying all day. I just didn't care. Grandma often reminded me I was going to be just like aunt Dottiea.

After my birthday I promised to study and quit hanging out. Everyday I began to catch the Swanson Home bus and be home studying. They could not believe the change I had made in the next six weeks. My grades went up to B.

My mind was changing. I had to get slicker and not get caught up in seeing things one way. Where there's a will there's a way. That song had been playing a long time in my head. I had to think for myself because my parents weren't around. Looking out for number one was the way to be.

"What the hell can anyone in here tell me?"

I was talking to one of my cousins. When another came inside and hollered at me.

"Samone, look who's outside..."

"Oh it's daddy. Hello daddy," I said running out to greet him.

He gave me a hug and a big kiss.

"You're going home with daddy."

I paused digesting the moment of happiness.

"We're leaving soon, okay."

"Okay."

He gave me fifty dollars and went inside the house. I went cross the railroad tracks to see Aunt Lane and my cousins.

"I'm leaving."

"Where're you going?"

"Back with my daddy..."

"That's good."

"Yep, I came to tell y'all."

"Are you gonna stay for the party?"

"I don't know..."

"Tuffie is gonna be there. You liked him."

"His fine self..." I thought aloud.

Tuffie was the only guy who moved me. And thank God he was not related.

"He's fine, Samone."

"Yeah, I might have to give him some before I leave."

"You be careful Samone, you know you don't take birth control pills."

"I know."

We started laughing. I walked down the other end of Ida Barbour and told Tuffie what was going on.

"Are you going with your fam?"

"Are you going with your girl?"

"Just meet me down here about eight, Samone. Eight, not ten minutes after eight, but eight o' clock, all right?"

Tuffie was eighteen. Full beard, football built, bowlegged, dark skin, not chocolate. I could hardly wait. I need to stop playing when it comes to boys. At the same time I wasn't going to let my emotions get played. I didn't like messing with boys with girlfriends. This was one exception. He was too fine. Eight o' clock please come quickly before I changed my mind.

That evening I went to the hang out spot, looking for Tuffie. Someone else greeted me.

"Hi Samone," one of his friends said.

"Where's Tuffie?"

"He went to the store, said he'd be right back."

"Hmm..." I was beginning to think that this was a mistake.

"You want to hit this joint?"

"Yeah," I said. "So what you been up to Moe?" I puffed.

"Out here, getting these things off..."

"I hear that."

"Me and Tuffie are the only ones holding today. He finished.  I gotta see a couple more customers then I'm through."

I never asked what they sold.  It really didn't make a difference.  He gave me what I asked for and that was good enough for me.

"Samone, what I tell you about smoking?"

It was Tuffie.

"Boy, I'm out of here tomorrow."

"Where you going, Samone?"

"To live with my daddy in DC," I said with a huge grin on my lips.

"Damn, I wish I could leave this dead ass city.  You're lucky as hell, Samone."

"Damn sure is," Tuffie said putting his arm around me and off we went.  As we walked through the fields someone was coming from the opposite direction. The person got closer then relief, we saw a big smile.  It was his brother CB.  I breathed a sigh because I thought it was his girlfriend.

When Tuffie and I reached his parents house the TV was on.  His father was up and his mother asleep.  We looked at each other shaking our heads.

"Hey dad, why don't you go to bed?"

"Yeah, I need too.  Goodnight."

The whole house was crowded.  Tuffie and I went in his room he started kissing me real hard, rubbing then fingering inside my legs and had my coochie throbbing like a toothache.

Damn, I thought, Kevin didn't carry on like this.  He was rubbing so much I was dripping.  He started taking off my clothes and tried to put it in.  He was huge.

"Ouch it hurts."

"Just let me put the head in, I'm going to go really slow."

That was all he could do. I couldn't take anymore.

"Get up. It hurts. Agh shit, take it out please," I begged.

"Samone be quiet. You want me to take it out for real, for real?"

"Yeah...! Hell yeah...!"

He wasn't so polite about it. He started forcing his hardness inside me.

"Relax and take this dick." He said and put his hand over mouth.

I struggled to breathe and he banged me so hard each stroke I felt in my lower belly. I was gonna suffer liver or spleen damage. He kept pounding and growling but there was only pain. I was sobbing and he thought it was sounds of pleasure.

"You like this dick, huh?" he groaned in my ear as he squirted.

Later we watched TV until ten. He put his arms around me and walked me home. He kissed me and gave me a key chain with Tuffie written on it.

"I'll come back every break and I'll stay for the summer." I said walking away.

As soon as I got in the door Aunt Dottiea was there, sniffing like a hound.

"Your daddy was looking for you he wanted to know had you packed," she said.

"I'm about to do that now." I answered running upstairs.

I was really dazed about what happened it felt like I was a

virgin. Tuffie gave it to me good and hard. Kevin never gave at like that at all. I thought rubbing my stomach. I was tired.

"Samone..."

"Uh..."

"Are you packing?" Aunt Dottiea asked.

"Yeah..."

"I'm going to fix you and your daddy a nice dinner before ya'll leave."

"Okay..."

I was ready to go. I couldn't wait to be off to the next adventure. What does it have to offer me? No more country life. I could have wasted my life away, to the point of being strung out. Only the strong survive.

I closed my eyes and thanked the Man up above for bringing me through my ordeal.

# 26

D.C.

In the elevator we got off at number 306. No company I can't believe that. I liked it when he had company. I'm not about to stay cooped up in here, I thought as I walked into his apartment.

"I'm going to give you five hundred dollars to go shopping and your Uncle Black says he's going to give you five hundred too," daddy said.

"All right, thanks daddy," I said with a big grin.

"You're a big girl, now. So make sure you get all the things you need and some personal hygiene products."

"Ok daddy."

"Daddy, can I take a walk go outside?"

"Sure," he smiled.

I walked outside smelling the city air. The bright lights were all around. People were out walking having fun. I thought about Mamacita and Shellie.  I would call them later, I decided.

I did what I was supposed to do in Lincoln Jr. High school.
I wore a suit the first day I entered and that set the tone.  I boldly
walked into my homeroom and introduced myself to the teacher,
Mr. Stevenson.

"Can you give me a second, Miss?" He asked.  I did and
checked out the class.  They were already staring and whispering.
One girl smiled and seemed friendly.  The boys they watched and
whispered.

"Class we have a new student.  Samone Johnson."

"She's a student?" The friendly girl said and the class
started laughing.  I sat down.  The same girl whispered: "We
thought you, were Stevenson's girlfriend.  You have on that suit
and... How old are you?"

"Sixteen..."

"For real...?"

"Yeah, I just like to wear suits."

"I know that's right.  I'm sorry, my name is Marina." The
Spanish girl said and introduced me to her friends.  They were
mostly Spanish.

"Class, please calm down.  I'm trying to get things cor-
rect."  Mr. Stevenson said.

"She's in all our classes."  Marina said as she looked at my
schedule.

"Why is that I don't have different classes from ya'll?"

"What school do you come from?"

"One year in Virginia fifteen years in Miami."

"Are you from Miami?"

"Yep…"

"Why you came here?"

"That's a long story, Marina."

First period was DC history, then math, followed by reading. At lunch, we left and went to the chicken spot down the block where a lot of students passed time. I glanced at the menu and saw some huge burger. We'd laughed at that in Miami. Every state specialized in some type of food.

English became my favorite subject thanks to p-town. It was at fourth period and Mrs. Shuler was the teacher. My first day she handed out prepositional phrases. Before she walked off, I had already read the directions.

"I'll explain," she said. "Oh, if anyone knows how to do it, then go ahead and begin."

I already knew how to do it. While Mrs. Shuler was explaining, I was on the second half. By the time she sat down to grade some papers, I was turning in my assignment.

"Let me see this."

She took the paper out of my hand and started grading it. Marina looked at me and smiled.

"You've got them all right too! Very good Samone I guess you do understand prepositions and prepositional phrases."

The next two classes were home economics and then typing. The whole homeroom had something to say about the teacher. She was mean and always fussing.

"Hi, are you a new student?" She asked when I sat in the class.

"Yes," I answered.

"What's your name, please?"

"Samone Johnson."

"Ms. Johnson do you have a schedule?"

"Yes…"

"May I see it please, I'm so used to seeing our students in jeans.  You're dressed up and you look nice."

"Thank you."

"Samone are you wearing another suit tomorrow?" Marina asked smiling.

"I might," I answered and we all laughed even Ms. Hook.

When I got home from the school the house was full of company.

"How was your day, Samone?"

"Fine thanks.  Daddy, we didn't have any homework. Could I go outside?"

"Sure…"

The game room was crowded with some cute boys.

"What's up Shortie, you new around here?"

"Yeah".

"What's your name?"

"Samone."

"Samone, you like love boat."

"It's all right when I don't watch."

"Watch, ah, ha, ha!"

"What's so funny what's-your-name?"

"I'm sorry, James, ha, ha, ha,"

"Why do you keep laughing at me, James?"

"You funny for real, you thought that I was talking about

the show."

"Yeah, what else could it be?"

"Love boat, it's some real deal. Something you smoke and will get you real high."

"Like weed?"

"Better, you'll be zooted into outer space. This some different shit," James smiled.

"Oh well, I don't want any of that. I'll take the weed."

"Where're you going?"

"To visit a friend," I said.

"All right, I'll see you again."

I walked out and I saw Bernice. She was walking with a young girl.

"Hello there, if it ain't Samone," Bernice said walking over to me.

"How're you doing?"

"Samone, this is my daughter, Janet. We are coming from therapy."

"Hi Janet," I said. She looked at me acting shy.

"Oh don't worry, it's not you. Janet is just is afraid of everyone. That's why she's in therapy. She was a victim of sex abuse at an early age. Her dad is your Uncle Black and he was a prime suspect. But he seemed to have bought his way out of it."

I stared at the little girl and felt all the compassion in my body reaching out to her. She was afraid of the world because of what she had experienced. Somewhere inside, I identified with the feeling, but it had an opposite effect on me. Bernice was speaking but I couldn't hear what she was saying. Her daughter's hollowed look behind sad eyes held me captive.  I understood.

"You should call this Victim rights attorney and she could tell you what to do to help."

On my way home my thoughts were burdened with the nightmare that Janet and Bernice was living.  How could you rape your own flesh and blood? Is that the reason he and my dad have been buttering me up with all these shopping sprees.  Was it hush money? I never figured out who had assaulted me.  No one ever asked me about it.  It was the biggest secret in the family.

I walked into the apartment and closed the door.  A party was in progress.  I went to the bedroom and as soon as I had lit the joint, I heard the knocking.

"Come in."

Daddy knocked then stuck his head in without waiting for an answer.

"I smell that?"

His girlfriends all started laughing.

"As long as you smoking in the house it's okay," daddy said.

"Samone, your daddy is cool," one of the girls said.

"This sure's some good weed, where you get this from?"

"A friend recommended this guy, James," I said.

"I can't stay inside when I smoke."

"Let's go to Fairmont basketball court they supposed to have a game today."

All this was really new to me.  This was the inner city. There was music and boys were balling.  They were all tall and fine.

One of daddy's girlfriend asked if I had a boyfriend. I told her about how I felt about Tuffie.

"Oh, I see. That's the name on your key chain."

I wanted to tell daddy about seeing Bernice. He was having a good time hanging out. I still couldn't get my mind off Janet.

Bernice said she was from p-town. That's where her and my daddy grew up. He had introduced her to Black and things were popping until Black came back from doing a bid in the state prison. Then he started acting different.

I was walking through the neighborhood when I saw James again.

"What's up Sam...ah...?"

"It's Samone, James," I said smiling.

"Yeah, your eyes look pretty."

All I could do was smile at his efforts.

"Samone, would you like to go-to the go-go?

"Boy, I don't do no go-go. What, you think I'm a stripper?"

"No, it ain't like that. Come with me."

We went to a party and the deejay started playing a song called; *Meet me at the Go-Go.*

They started doing a dance called the 'happy feet'. It was live and everyone was having a good time.

"Everybody go to the go-go here. Where you from, ya'll go to the Go-Go?"

"No, we go to the skating rink, baby. That's our thing."

The Go-Go was the shit as far as D.C., but for Miami I was just fine with the rink. Everybody in D.C. wore tennis shoes. That was cute for them. Me, I liked colors. My shirt and shoes, I like them to match.

I was having a good old time with James when I saw Bernice. She came over and started yelling at me. She seemed drunk and I wasn't having it. I walked away. James tried to talk both of us out of fighting. Then his girl wound up coming along and cut me with a razor blade.

Blood covered the brand new coat that my daddy had just bought me. This bitch cut me and left me bleeding like a pig.

"Bitch, I'm going to kill you!" I screamed.

The more blood came, the more I was trying to fight her. She cut me again but I was still swinging.

"Samon, stop. You're bleeding. We got to get you to a hospital."

"No, fuck this blood! Bitch come back, let's fight!"

I ran after her and fell, a man picked me up.

We were on 15th and Euclid. I found out that she lived just around the corner from Malcolm X Park. Blood was everywhere.

Before I knew it I was in Children's Hospital getting stitched-up. The left side of my temple ached.

"She was very lucky that her eyes were unharmed." The doctor said.

My father's girlfriends helped me. He was on his way home. He said Uncle Black would be calling soon.

I heard the keys turning in the locks.

"Hi baby you all right?"

"Yeah, she just cut me I beat her with the heel of my shoe.

Then I chased her with a stick before she cut me."

"Samone, there's ice on the ground."

"I know. When I'm mad I don't feel nothing. Plus my shoes made me slip so I had to take them off, and what the hell might as well use it upside her head. If Bernice wasn't there..."

"Bernice, what was she doing there?"

"She had a nerve to say I can fight. Daddy, she was a big girl. She had to get the shoe."

"Are you all right baby?"

"Yeah daddy, I just have a headache. They gave me something for it."

"My friend, Carmen is going to stay here. I gotta go back to Baltimore. Uncle Black is going to call you, okay?"

It was puzzling me that Uncle Black wanted to call. I decided not to ask daddy why and waited for Uncle Black to call. Daddy also stayed in Baltimore. I visited before and met my stepsister, Diamond Johnson. Daddy started staying in Baltimore a lot. Every time Mamacita called, he was there. I was in the house seven days a week. Daddy was there for two.

I went to school. James and I hung at the Go-Go every weekend. It was fun watching all the bands do battle. They had crews Park Road and Gangster Chronicles. Most of boys wore high top fades. Some were the pretty boy type, they were from 7th and T. I had three favorite Go-Go bands, Pump Blenders, EU Chuck Brown and the Soul Searchers.

You can tell when everyone had a good weekend at Lincoln Jr. High. They all came back beating drum on their desks. Homeroom became off-the-hook. I had gotten a little looser myself.

I stopped snorting coke. After I got cut, I never did it again. I asked daddy about love-boat.

"Never smoke it." He warned.

Uncle Black told me to give him the girl's name that had cut me. I delayed and he began pressing me for it.

"That's all you've got to do and it'll be a done deal."

"It was just a fight and she cut me. James went looking for her. He couldn't find her and that's his girlfriend."

When daddy came by, I told him about Uncle Black.

"Uncle Black is trying to get her killed?"

"Yeah, he sure is. All he needs is her name."

"Daddy, my stitches healed. You can't tell that I had stitches. It looks like scratches, so the next time Uncle Black calls or comes by, I'll tell him we already took care of it, okay, daddy?"

"All right, I'm going over Baltimore this weekend. You want to go?"

"No daddy, I'll be fine right here."

The weekend went by with no further incident. Uncle Black came by and left saying he was going to Baltimore to meet up with my dad. I went to school that Monday morning with a fresh outlook on life. I definitely didn't want to tangle with any other girl over their boyfriends.

"Good morning, Samone."

"Good morning, Marina."

"Hey Samone, we were planning on going over a friend's house for lunch."

"Oh you're talking about the one who always be wearing

those nice pair of boots."

"Yeah, she's fly," she said.

Later that evening I was home doing homework and heard the door. It was Carmen and Uncle Black. She walked into the bedroom.

"Daddy's gone for the week, huh?" she asked.

"You want to come over by me?"

"Maybe tomorrow," I said.

"I'll leave the number before I go."

"I'll call you tomorrow." Uncle Black hollered as he left.

"Ok, goodnight, Uncle Black," I said.

"Okay..."

Black and Carmen must have run into each other.

The week went by and I made the best of time, doing homework and watching television. I was taking easy short strolls through the Zoo and around the block. I never saw James. The weekend came and I saw Carmen again. After she had left I heard keys turning in the door. This time Uncle Black came in alone.

"Samone..."

"Huh?"

"What's up, baby?"

"Nothing..."

"You're in here alone on a Friday night?"

"Yeah, not a whole lot to do."

"Your daddy left you?"

"I didn't see him before he left.

"He knew I was coming by."

"He won't be back until Monday."

"Monday...!"

He handed me two crisp one hundred dollar bills plus a fifty.

"Remember your Uncle is always got you, alright?"

"Yeah..."

"Go across the street and see what's playing at the Ontario."

"Ok..."

I took a long hot shower. Uncle Black was still in the kitchen. It sounded like he was sifting something. I wanted to take another peek, but I didn't like the way he was sitting. He could easily have spotted me. I walked straight back to the bed-room.

"Samone, I'm getting ready to leave, I'll be over at the club if you need me."

"Ok..."

"Are you going to the movies?"

"Yep, Uncle Black you know what's playing?"

"I took the back way home. I don't have a clue. It might be Scar Face."

"Oh yeah, Aunt Dottiea was talking about that movie."

"Something else is playing but I don't recall. I'm gone."

"All right, thanks Uncle Black."

I got to carry a big purse so I can go to Chun Shun and get some shrimp fried rice. This night was going to be all right, Scare Face, Chinese food and a joint. I knew daddy got some stashed.

Monday morning came quickly. It was chilly, the end of October. There had been warm weather up until today. The ringing phone disturbed my thoughts. Who was calling this early in the morning? I wondered as I answered.

"Hello...Hi good morning daddy. Getting ready for school...Some money, yes...All right daddy, see you tomorrow."

It didn't matter how long he stayed away. I was used to it now. I got money for the bills and food was always in the house. I was fine.

My first report card was good. I had A in science, B in DC history, B in math, B in English, A in reading, B in PE. The only D was in typing.

"That's the best report card I had since Elementary." I told Marina.

I went home happy and lit a joint. I hadn't felt happy like this in awhile. Daddy took care of whatever he had to take care of. That was how it went down. I was cool with it. There was nothing like peace, quiet and time out for self.

School was nice but every day after school I would see this young man standing outside the school. I could feel him staring at me and in the beginning I didn't pay him a whole lot of attention. By the second week, we were making eye contact. Monday he was outside at lunchtime. He was staring real hard at me.

"Marina there goes that boy I was telling you about."

"Where...?" she asked, glancing in the wrong direction.

"Right over there. Watch this."

"What're you looking at?"

"You," he answered boldly.

"All right why don't you stop staring and come tell me your name."

"Damn! He's got a nice bod too," Marina said.

"Hi, how're you doing?"

"Fine and you...?"

Marina started laughing.

"That's Marina and I'm Samone."

"I'm Randy."

"You don't attend school here, do you?"

"No I don't."

"But you're up here everyday."

"Yeah I see you too."

"Well, it's lunchtime we're going to the chicken spot."

"All right give me your number before you step."

I wrote it down. Marina and I walked off.

"Samone, you're all right with me, girl."

"What?"

"That's the shit I'm talking about. You asked the boy what he looking at."

"He was staring on a regular. I just wanted to make sure he wasn't stalking me."

"I saw the look."

"Child please, just because I wear suits and do my work don't make me a nerd."

I took Marina over to my house and cooked lunch. That girl was a kid for real. She took her shoes off and started jumping on the bed smiling. I didn't mind. She was just having fun. Later she settled down and we spoke.

"Where's your father?"

"Baltimore, girl, I'm always home by myself."

"Not me. Three sisters, one brother and my mother plus my stepfather, I'm gonna have to start coming over your house."

"I don't care."

We hurried back to school. When school let out, I saw Randy, waved and was on my way home. The phone rang when I was in.

"Hello..."

It was Randy. We talked for about two hours. He had no school tomorrow, it was a teachers' workday.

I called Carmen to see what she was doing. She invited me over and I went and was chilling. Her other friends stopped by. We smoked joint after joint. As soon as one went out, another was passed to me. I started puffing, I smacked my lips and it didn't taste like weed.

"Carmen is this boat?"

"Yeah love-boat," she answered.

I hit it again puffing, inhaling and passing it.

"Do you want some more, Samone?"

I hit it again even harder than before. Sucking in my cheeks and filling my lungs with the blue smoke. I passed it, sitting in an easy chair and looking out the window. Before I knew it, I was stuck, caught in a twilight zone. My face felt like it was expanding.

"I need to lie down." I suddenly blurted.

From that moment, I began pacing back and forth to the bathroom, checking my face out. I touched it, to make sure that it was the right size. It felt like my face had expanded from left to right. I kept touching my face and looking in the mirror. My eyes saw one thing but my mind was saying something different I went and laid back down, still feeling my face.

"Why did ya'll let me smoke that boat?"

"You wanted to…"

"My daddy told me not to smoke that stuff. I had some nerve hittin' that shit. Why ya'll give me that shit."

"Get some milk." Someone said.

"No, I don't want any."

"Wanna walk to Wendy's?"

"Yeah, let me get myself together first."

When we made it to Wendy's, I made sure I got a large Frosty. By the time we got back to Carmen's house, I was feeling better.

"I'm never smoking that boat again. Don't offer me any. And from now on let me know what it is, I thought it was a damn joint." I scolded Carmen.

# 27 NASTY BOYS

Randy and I had gotten very close. Daddy found out. He took me to the doctor because I kept complaining about my ache on my left side. It was a result of ovulation. When the nurse asked if I was a virgin, I wanted to say yes.

She spoke to daddy. Then I was given a battery of tests and a three-month supply of pills. Daddy and I walked home he walked in front of me and didn't say a word. He was acting funny. Then it hit me. That damn nurse must've told him.

Randy and I talk half the night away. He made plans to come. Daddy wouldn't be there. I was asleep when someone was knocked.

"Who is it?"

"Randy," I opened the door. "How did you get in the building?"

"Some lady let me in."

I went in the bathroom. He followed.

"Can I wash my face and brush my teeth please? You can go in my room."

I came out the bathroom and sat next to Randy. He started kissing me, laid me back on my pillow and was taking his shoes off while still kissing me. Then he was taking my underwear off. Before I knew it, Randy was poking me with his dick.

He felt the tightness and a big smile covered his handsome face. He started to gently rock back and forth, really slow. It hurt and felt real good, not like it did with Tuffie. Randy started really getting down in it, moving his hips faster and faster. Even though Tuffie was more passionate, I was enjoying Randy far more. After we were finished, I showered and went to school.

That night when Randy and I were on the phone, the first thing he wanted to know was when we were going to do it again. I slept with him a few more times but I was not feeling Randy. We drifted apart although I really like the way he did his thing.

"The only reason that Randy got with you was because you started having sex with him."

"That may be true but that phase is over."

Later, I spent time at Carmen's and her friends again. Sure thing they tried to get me to smoke that shit again.

"She dipped that cigarette in the boat juice again?"

"I don't know..." Carmen's friend said.

"I told her I never want that shit. I found out that they use embalming fluid to make it. That's why my face felt like it was about two feet on both sides." I said and they all laughed.

One evening when daddy and all his female friends were over the house they were in the kitchen. Carmen seemed real high. She began talking to me.

"Carmen you love that shit. You're too young to be doing it all the time. You gonna get hooked on that shit."

Carmen sat next to me in the bedroom. This is what they called shit-faced, back home. She looked as if she wanted to cry.

"You know you smoked this before. I was here once when your Uncle Black gave you some."

"Uncle Black would never give me that."

"Who you think turned me on to it?"

"I don't know..."

"You came here, when you were about eleven or twelve. I was fifteen or sixteen. Your Uncle came back here and gave some to you then he took your virginity."

The words stumbled out of her mouth in a slow manner. It was as if the weight they carried slurred her speech. She looked at the disbelief written on my face and nodded.

"He did."

"You're crazy. Stop using that shit."

"We are just mules. And these pads, your daddy and Black owns about six between the two of them. I could tell you something else about Bernice and her daughter, but I can see that you're not ready for it."

She walked out leaving me stunned and went in the bathroom. Carmen came out and walked to the living room. In her back pocket, I saw a syringe needle. What the fuck was that doing in her pocket? I knew damn well, they're not doing that. My daddy! These people are supposed to be his friends.

I went out that night and walked feeing the chill of autumn winds. Thinking about what Carmen had told me, I wasn't myself.

Christmas was around the corner. Daddy called and said he had a car accident. His car was totaled and there was a lawsuit. I went to visit him.

"Your mother wants you to come home for Christmas. You should go. She misses you," he said when I was leaving. I wanted to ask about Bernice but it seemed inappropriate. She hadn't been around lately. Maybe she went back to p-town.

The news about going back to Mamacita dogged me on the ride back to DC. I knew she was going to start something.

I was convinced that there was no way to prevent a duel between Mamacita and myself. Heading back home on the plane, my mind was on edge. Mamacita and Shellie picked me up from the airport. We hugged and I wondered if this was all for show.

I called Yolanda to let her know that I was back in town. Mamacita and Shellie had moved from Opalocka back to Carol City. The new house was really nice.

"Look at your hands. They're not dark anymore. They're nice and brown," Mamacita said without any prompting.

I didn't understand that. What, she didn't like me because I was dark skin? What was really going on?

They got a kick out of me while I was in the mirror putting on my eyeliner. Both were laughing and talking about how much I'd grown. The next day, I caught the bus to Opalocka and ran into Kevin. He had the biggest smile on his face.

"Samone, Samone, where you been?"

"I don't live here anymore. I moved to DC with my father."

"You sound like you white, girl."

"Stop playing, for real."

"Where're you going?"

"Over to Yolanda's."

I gave him my number and told him to call later.

Yolanda and I hugged.

"Look at you, girl. You look good. I know you glad you left."

"Okay girl, I'm having a ball."

"So you have a new boyfriend, right?"

"I had one, Randy. But he's history. He was too immature."

"Okay," she said.

"I need somebody that has a car."

"Right, I heard you."

"Girl, guess who I just saw?"

"Who...?"

"Kevin..."

"For real...?"

"Where you seen him at?"

"On the avenue and I gave him my new number."

"Ol' Kevin..."

"Right..."

Yolanda and I headed to the Flea Market.

"So what're you going to get?"

"Some jewelry, playgirl ring, and another ring with my

initials, some jeans and whatever else they have. Daddy gave me two hundred and fifty dollars. Plus I had some saved from before."

"Okay, your daddy's nice. You got spoiled. How's the ol' girl acting?"

"She looked at my hands and said how light they are."

"What's up with that?"

"What's up with that? Yolanda if I find out, I'll let you know."

"She's still tripping huh?"

"Must be..."

We hung at the flea market talking shit and shopping. Then later I went home. Kevin called the next day. He wanted to come by and thought he could get some pussy. He was in for a rude awakening. When I told him no, he acted kind a funny and I knew that would be the last time I heard from him. I didn't care, I don't roll like that. Kevin left with an attitude and never called back. I was going to call and tell Yolanda about it but Shellie wanted to use her phone.

"Can you wait?" I asked.

"It's my phone and I want to use it now. You don't live here anymore."

Before she could say another word, I smacked her right in the face with the receiver.

"I'm going to tell." She cried running off.

She was crying and yelling at the same time. I heard Mamacita say that she was going to have to drink the whole time I was there.

I called my daddy and told him that I was ready to come

home.

"First of all, when I get here she started with how light my hands are. She didn't let me go out for Christmas. Shellie told me it was her phone, get off it so I popped her in the face with the phone. I hear Mamacita saying she just going to stay drunk until I leave."

Later that night, Mamacita called me in the living room.

"You probably ready to go home."

"Yes, I am."

"You like living with your daddy?"

"Yep, I go shopping and always have money. Go out with no fuss, and come in with no fuss."

"Samone, I didn't send you up there to have a good time. I sent you up there to teach you a lesson."

I could not believe this woman.

"You brought over three hundred dollars here and spent it all. You didn't even think to buy me a gift."

"My father gave money to me for me. I'm sleepy. I'm going to bed."

"I'm not through with you."

"May I be excused? Please, good night."

# 28

I left for my daddy's home back in DC and started the New Year on a better note.    Daddy was still running back and forth to Baltimore.

One night, Uncle Black came over and was in the kitchen. On this occasion I was in the living room when he walked in.

"Hi Samone..."

"Hi Uncle Black..."

"What you up to?"

"Not a lot."  I answered and heard him cursing.

"Samone you know who's been under this cabinet?"

"Carmen and her friends..."

"That bitch back in Baltimore.  They need to stop fucking with my shit!"

I waited for about fifteen minutes and went in the kitchen

faking like I wanted something to drink. On the table were these bars looking like soap. Uncle Black was busy putting some of this and a little of that into measuring cups. Then weighing and placing it in small bags. I drank three cups of juice while observing. Then I left and went to the bedroom. I fell on the bed.

Drugs! That was where all the money came from. That was how I'm able to get all that money. Uncle Black is the pusher-man.

Daddy's new girlfriend Regina and I had gotten close. She would talk to me and take me shopping every time the Baltimore crew came over. She told me who was sleeping together. Of the four women that used to come over, my father was sleeping with all of them, sometimes all at once. The story that slapped me in the face was when she told me, my father had been shooting heroin in his feet. My whole world felt like it was going to crumble.

She mentioned that my father was going to buy me a Rolex for my seventeenth birthday and he did. I knew she could be trusted. I asked her about Bernice.

"Bernice's a crazy ass. She using her daughter to try and get at Black," she said.

"Where's Bernice?"

"She got paid off and left the District."

"Good for Bernice."

I met an older guy that went by the name, Carefree. He hung out at school in the afternoon and was always playing basketball. Carefree stayed up the school and was always calling my house. We used to meet up at the Go-Go. Sometimes he would spend the night. He was twenty-one and a real cutie. All the girls went goo-goo over him. I found out that he had a daughter and his baby's mother was not happy about hearing that he was spending time with me.

One night after a basketball game, Marina and I were walking. Carefree's baby's mother passed me and I heard her utter the word "bitch." She repeated it, and we got into a verbal altercation.

She called her peoples. I ran down the street to the house with Marina following me. I went straight to the drawer, found the gun and started loading it.

"Samone, are you crazy, girl? What're you doing?" Marina asked with a strained looked on her face.

"I'm not getting cut anymore and I refuse to have some bitches try and jump me." I said making sure the rounds were in.

Marina dialed Carefree's number. By the time I reached the front door. Carefree was on the telephone.

"Hello... you better come get your baby mother..."

I threw the gun on the bed, and ran down the stairs with my razor blade under my tongue. Carefree's baby mamma was outside. All of a sudden, these cars started pulling up. She had brought her brother. Carefree and his brother showed up.

"Why you call him, huh?" his baby-mama asked.

"I didn't call nobody."

'Samone, please go upstairs."

"Tame your bitch," I warned.

Marina was scared. Carefree came upstairs and saw the gun on the bed.

"Oh, you were for real," he said.

"I'll kill that bitch. She needs to find someone else to fuck with. I'm not the one."

"I know. That's why I came right away. Man, you gonna have to get a grip, Samone."

"No, you need to check her. She started this thing."

Carefree left and went home. He called back later and we chatted on the phone half the night.

After that Ms. Baby-mother would call often. She knew Carefree was with me now.

Drugs were big money game. I kept hearing about crack, and half of the girls wanted a boyfriend that was a dealer. It wasn't a big deal to have a hustler boyfriend. My daddy and uncle sold heroin and I didn't want for nothing. They say don't get high on your own supply but I guess daddy knew what he was doing.

Regina started coming over a lot. Most of the times, she would be in the room with me until daddy wanted her. I liked Regina. We would sit and talked about girly stuff. I told her about the situation when I first came here. She thought I did right by not telling anyone, because I didn't know who had molested me anyway.

"Your daddy would've killed the sonnofabitch," she said.

"Samone, I'm going down 11th and O. You want to hang?" daddy asked.

"No, I'm going to do my homework."

"What about you, Regina?"

"I'll stay with Samone."

"See y'all when I get back."

The phone rang and I picked it up. It was for daddy. He

told me to take a message.

"Daddy, who's Kaderia?" I asked.

"She's from Portsmouth. Her mother lived at the other end of Ida Barbour." He answered and walked out.

"She used to work for a construction company and hurt her back on the job. Her lawsuit settlement is in." Regina said.

"That's good."

"She has a daughter named Kadeia and a son, Rasheed. They're Muslims."

"For real...?"

"For real, they only eat fish and vegetarian foods."

"Regina what part of town they live?"

"Southwest..."

"I like all the high-rise." I said looking out the window.

"This is called the Wingate."

They all returned with daddy, Rasheed had pretty braids.

"Rasheed and Kadeia meet your sister, Samone." Daddy said.

"Hello, how are you?"

"Fine and yourself...?"

When we went back in the room Kadeia said: "I thought that you would be red like me."

"How could you say that?" Rasheed asked.

"I'm dark skinned and so is daddy Earl." I said.

Bitch, that's not your father, I thought. But I remembered that was the only father they knew.

We left and went shopping. That was always fun.

First time in any part of Jersey, they had no tax. Two-tone

jeans with matching jean jackets are hot for the city. That's all I saw that I wanted. I'll save the rest for the mall.

Carefree in the meantime, had found a crew to hustle for him. They were all young boys.

Once Kadeia found us, she was over every weekend. She even started eating red meat.

"Oh, so you can eat red meat now?"

"Mommy said it was okay. I had forgotten to tell you. Carefree said that he coming over."

"Well, he can come over all he wants. I'm going to the Black Hole to see Chuck Brown and the Soul Searchers."

I'm sick of his ass always trying to stop me from going to the Go-Go. Before I gave him some, that nigga used to do as I say. Now that he had me and felt how tight it was, he wanted to do it every time I see him. He even started sizing my body up talking about how my ass is looking more luscious than before. It hurt every time we did it. I'm not tripping. I was out.

WHAT'S A
GIRL TO DO?

# 29

Two summers had gone by and Carefree was still around. Marina's friendship faded away. I can't tell the last time I've seen her. Regina still was paying all the bills. Uncle Black kept my pockets stacked. One night Carefree called looking for some. I declined.

"What's wrong?" he asked.

"Nothing..."

"Since you're at Dunbar you think you're all that, Samone. You aren't Dunbar material."

"Carefree what is it? Are you on your period? What're you calling my house for?"

"Where is your father?"

"I think you can answer that question."

"You want me to keep you company?"

"If that's what you wanted to do that's all you had to say.

Don't call here trying to aggravate me. I'm sick of your shit anyway. You tried to run me over cause I went to the Go-Go. Then you had the nerve to put Marina and me out your car."

"If you think that I'm going to sit up there and let ya'll two motherfuckas sit in my ride and talk about how y'all party, you crazy."

"Oh really...?"

"I'm supposed to be your boyfriend and you side with some guy that's on his own."

"Oh well, I don't need you to do anything for me my uncle and my daddy hold it down. So whatever you do is cause you want to, I don't ask you for shit..."

"Samone, you know you love me."

"Sometimes, but you switch up too much."

"When you first came, you used to be so nice. Now you act just like a DC girl."

"Oh, well look, are you coming over here or what?"

"You cook...?"

"Yeah...Why are you hungry?"

"Yeah..."

"You bake a cake?"

"Sure did."

"With lemon icing...?"

"Yep..."

"All right, I'll be there in a little while."

He hung up and the phone rang again.

"Hello?"

"Hey Samone..."

"Hi daddy..."

"I'll be over there tomorrow, okay?"

"See you tomorrow, daddy."

All of a sudden there was knocking on the door.

"Who is it?"

"Me..."

"Damn, thought you said in a little while."

"I was in the neighborhood. Is the food warm?"

"Not yet, why? I just got off the phone with my father."

"He should have millions the way he stays in Baltimore."

The quiet storm hummed softly on the radio. Anita Baker was rolling like it was her birthday. Next up; Teddy, then it was Luther's turn. I was blown away and before I knew it, I was naked. My legs wide open and feeling passionate kisses from my lips to my neck.

"Do you love me?" I asked.

"Yes I do," he replied.

Carefree was sucking so hard on my neck, I knew a passion mark would be a reminder. He was inserting his penis and just before the head touched my throbbing lips, I was too busy too thinking whether or not I had taken my pills.

"Ah...ooh ...I didn't take my...oh baby... pill..."

I was not in control of the situation. My legs tingled and my toes curled.

"I thought you said it made you sick."

His fingers played with the entrance to my love canal. It was throbbing and wet. He ignored my weak protests and began riding me juicy all night. I exploded in clmax after climax.

Morning came with him feeling all over me. We had an encore session. I showered.

"Carefree, stop trying to grab my ass and drop me off at Margaret Washington," I said as I dressed.

"Margaret Washington...?"

"Yeah, I go there in the morning..."

"I thought you went to Dunbar?"

"I do, in the afternoon."

Carefree did and slapped my ass as I got out the car.

"See you later shortie."

At lunchtime we saw all the hustlers outside hitting up customers for lunch. They profiled in 190e Mercedes and stunted in kitted Maximas. Those with BMWs weren't just flossing, they had real money.

I thought about Marina. We had been close until a girl had stabbed her in the head with a pair of scissors. She hadn't been around for couple weeks.

I decided to walk to Popeye's chicken. There was Marina with her hair shaved around the sides and a Mohawk like she Punky Brewster.

"Girl you crazy," I said on seeing her.

I'll never forget the day she came to homeroom, jumped through the door talking about her new name was Queen Philly. She was serious too. That day she wore different color tennis shoes. She started break-dancing on the floor.

I walked to O street market with her to get a steak and cheese. They had the best ones in town.

"Girl, Carefree better not pick me up from school today."

"Why?"

"I don't want to keep riding in that green machine.  He needs to take it to a body shop.  The sides looks like it should be in the haunted house."

"You know you like him, Samone."

"He's all right, but the time I went away for the summer, he got him a girlfriend while I was away.  It haven't been the same, I've lost a lot of respect for him."

"Yeah I feel you."

"That hurt.  He's the only one that I sleep with.  Shit I wish I could give it to Ruffin."

We both laughed.

That evening I opened the door and I saw daddy with two women naked on the sofa.  I went to my room and closed the door. He was making a lot of money, we could afford more than this one bedroom.  Two women, he was a bad motherfucker.  Later I went to the kitchen and seated there was Uncle Black.

"Hi Uncle…"

"Hey Samone…"

I watched him for a minute, next thing I found myself at the table helping to bag shit up.  It made my adrenalin pump.  I felt like I was putting work in.  I saw the whole morning program. Dope is boy, and there was b, k. and a.  Heroin so crystal clear looked like fish scales.

It came shipped in looking like a bar of soap.  With swift, gentle strokes, Uncle Black was filling the table with snow.  He used measuring spoons, then he lifted Reynolds wrap and placed the boy in a bag.  He sealed the bag with tape.

Uncle Black worked in silence. He sent me to the store. When I returned, he was finished.

"Here Samone, thanks." He said and gave me two hundred dollars. Quick money, I thought smiling.

Over the next couple weeks things remained the same. I began innocently assisting Uncle Black with the preparation of his product. I'd get so much money, I shopped whenever I wanted. I was at the mall when I started feeling dizzy. Carefree couldn't be reached. I called Marina and she helped me. Following day she told me that Carefree was at the Go-Go.

"I told Carefree you were sick."

"Girl, fuck his tired ass."

"He started to tell me something but the music was too loud, I couldn't hear him."

The phone began ringing.

"Hello...Hi Bernice...no one is here...I haven't seen either of them in weeks...I will...okay. I don't want to talk to the DA...no bye."

I had lied. I had seen both daddy and Uncle Black. Bernice was back. She wanted me to talk to the DA about being pregnant. What would be the use of that? I had other things to worry about. I called Marina.

"I need you to go to plan parenthood with me." I said. "I didn't...Yep Carefree is going to trip out."

That evening when we met she told me about the happenings.

"You know Carefree talking shit since he got a rack of coke."

"Girl, fuck him! He makes me so sick.  He thinks he king-pin and pimp daddy rolled into one."

"He sez that somebody told him you messin' round with some guy named, D."

"That's my fucking business! So what...?"

"You know the first thing he's going to say if you pregnant is that ain't my baby.  You know how petty he can get."

Marina was right.  If I was pregnant hopefully I wasn't.

"When are you going for the results?"

"Saturday..."

"That's tomorrow."

"Right..."

"Well shit I might as well pack my bags.  And stay over."

"That's cool, I'm by myself."

Saturday we both went to the clinic.  I was a little nervous.

"Ms. Johnson..."

"Yes..."

"Here are the results."

"What did they say Samone?" Marina anxiously asked.

"Damn Samone."

"I know...double damn."

"Are you going to get an abortion?"

"I'm too scared."

On the way back all I was thinking was that my daddy was going to have a fit.

Months went by and I didn't say a word to anyone.  After awhile it became impossible for me to button my clothes.  Everyday I was getting sick and I began gaining a lot of weight.  Mamacita called and I broke down and told her.

"You want me to tell your daddy?" she asked.

"Would you?"

"What's the number over Baltimore?"

Mamacita hung up the phone.

Two days later Mamacita called back after speaking to him. Daddy had a problem with being a grandfather at such an early age. He had asked if I wasn't on birth control. She told him they made me sick.

"He called you?"

"No, I called back and found that they never gave him the message. He was mad but then after awhile he calmed down. He has a problem about being a grandfather."

Mamacita and I spoke often and we were getting close. She called and checked to make sure I was alright. She told me to eat crackers and suck lemons for morning sickness. That helped. After awhile, the sickness was gone. I hardly saw Daddy and Uncle Black stayed away. I mean they dropped me like a hot potato.

Money and food were getting low. Regina came over and paid the bills. She gave me some money. Daddy was in town, but never bothered to come see me. He called on the phone. He was too busy. I was pissed.

I continued attending school. I had to get a job and took one at McDonalds so I could buy groceries. Money was definitely funny. Daddy and Uncle Black fell back. Carefree was an asshole. That bitch-ass nigga came to my job with his crew and showed his stink ass.

"I ain't ya baby father," he said.

My co-workers heard him say that shit and they all looked at me. Then his friend came to the register and ordered. This nigga looked me up and down then called me a bum-ass bitch.

"You know that ain't my man's baby. You were fucking with D."

"Your mother is a bum ass bitch!" I screamed.

"Samone..." one of my coworkers said.

I had to catch myself. I didn't want to stoop to his level.

Alone at home, the phone rang. It was Kaderia telling me that she heard I was pregnant. She promised to come by and take me to a doctor she knew.

I found that I was twelve weeks pregnant. Kaderia paid for the visit. I spoke to my daddy. He told me to go to the Marie Reed clinic, it was free. My prenatal care started.

By Spring I was showing but not much. Regina came and paid the rent and kept me company. Daddy stayed away.

One evening, I went in the basement to put my clothes in the dryer. A man was there.

"Do you have the time?" he asked.

"No," I answered and kept it moving.

I closed the laundry door behind me and head for the elevator after putting my clothes in the dryer. I was getting on the elevator when, out of nowhere, I was surprised by a person in black ski mask. He started pulling at me and I grabbed onto the laundry door. He was stronger and pulled me so hard that eventually my fingers were pried from the doorknob.

He pushed me in the dark trash room. This bastard could

see my stomach but started pushing me against an opaque glass window. I kept screaming as the low-life tried his best to assault me in the basement. Every woman should have a weapon. I would've killed this fucking bastard.

When I got inside the apartment, I was crying and called the police. Half hour went by before two officers showed up. Kaderia came by and called every now and then. Daddy never returned my call.

I wasn't really happy but I understood. I called again and his baby's mother answered the phone. I told her to tell him I need him to come and stay with me.

A half an hour later, he called, ranting.

"What do you mean I have to *come* stay with you? I don't have to do nothing and I'm not coming over there."

"All right," I said and hung up the phone.

I didn't see daddy until I had a baby boy eight pounds four ounces. Kevin Garnet Johnson, named after my first love, Kevin. I didn't see anymore but he had been kind to me and I always remembered kindness. He was the first one to visit. Daddy gave me money and told me he would be in Baltimore if I needed him. I stayed in the hospital for five days because of a C-section.

Marina told Carefree I had the baby. I had gone into labor while she was visiting me. Carefree bought her a lot of balloons for me.

My son had to stay in the hospital after I was discharged. Carefree's mother visited, she took a look at my son and swooned.

"That's my grandson," she smiled.

My son became the most precious thing in my life. Eventually, Carefree came around and visited. His mother must've told him the baby looked just like him.

When school started I took Kevin to school with me. Carefree took care of Kevin when he felt like. Once in a while daddy came around.

Dunbar had a daycare so I pretty much had it mapped out. Kevin received clothes and the cupboard stocked with his formula.

Uncle Black called to wish me well. I guess that meant he wasn't mad at me anymore.

Thank God for WIC or sometimes I would've gone really crazy. I don't have to depend on anyone. I mean nobody especially my raggedy ass baby father walking around with two thousand in his pocket giving his baby's mothers a hard time about some small piece of change. He was a stingy ass running around town stunting.

Carmen came back around after hearing about the baby. The only problem was she brought her addiction with her.

"Come on try it." She encouraged me one day. "All you got to do is bend your head back and light it. Then you say beam me up Scotty." She laughed.

"This thing is trying to get me strung out. I don't think so."

I was depressed and tried it. I started selling it to all Carmen's friends. I didn't want to be in the drug game, but it kept dragging me in.

I used the money to make sure me and my son were straight. I was always buying him outfits. Then I'd go get my hair did. We had lunch money and carfare to get back and forth to school.

Carmen would come by and I would hit the pipe with her and give her the supply. She told Uncle Black what I was doing. I was home one day, high as hell when he called. The next day he came by and saw me.

"Oh by the way, your father told me to tell you, if you don't stop he's going to have to put you out."

"He got some nerves he sells drugs and I can't, no one is really helping me like that anymore."

One day I came home from school and an eviction notice was on the door. When Carmen came over, I showed it to her.

"Did you call your father?"

"No I'll call now," I said and picked up the phone. "Hi is my daddy there? No...could you tell him to call me. It's an emergency. There was an eviction notice on the door..."

I could not believe what was going on. Why didn't he pay the rent? Damn an eviction notice. The phone disturbed my agitated thoughts. The answer was even more damaging.

"Samone, your father told me to tell you, he don't know what to tell you..."

# 30    NOT ANOTHER MINUTE

I paced back and forth.  I was at a loss, going dizzy, wondering who I could call.  I thought about Mamacita but the last time I spoke to her about my light bill, I hung up before we got into it.  Every time I called her asking for help she would start an argument.  Even with that I decided to call.  Maybe I was just setting myself up.

"Hello Mamacita…I came home from school and found an eviction notice on the door.  I was trying to explain to you about the light bill and you tried to start an argument…he told one of his flunkies to tell me 'he don't know what to tell me.'  The rent is two hundred and seventy eight dollars…I don't know.  I'll talk to you later.  I need to make some calls."

My heart sank with the click.  I hung up thinking why did I  set myself up for her bullshit.  Mamacita can cancel me out for

anything. She spent my money. I mean all of it, from my dancing and she doesn't have two hundred and seventy-eight dollars.

I called my no-good baby daddy. All he did was offer
advice and then had the nerve to say because I had a child, the government wouldn't put me out on the streets. Fuck him.

My next move was to call my cousins. Lucky for me I had
kept in touch with some of them. I started going down the list of
the ones who I had been in touch with. I spoke to each of them
hoping for a positive answer.

The following week, I went to court. I thought everything
was under control until I found out that the rent was six months
behind. You could have bought me for a wooden nickel. What's
really going on? How was I supposed to come up with the fifteen
hundred and sixty dollars and the late fees? There was no one
around to give me any money. My family had turned their backs
on me.

I went to the welfare center after court. I had to do something. This was more than an emergency. I filled out document
after document and my caseworker immediately called the rental
office to put a stay on the eviction. She came back saying that the
court had rescheduled the hearing. I had another seventy two
hours.

"Ms. Johnson it's a good thing that you came in today or
you and your son would've been on the streets."

I didn't say anything because my facial expression said it
all.

"Where's your father?"

"I don't know. The last time I heard something from him

was a couple weeks ago."

"I'm sorry to hear that Ms. Johnson. That's unfortunate news. I have to send an investigator out to your home to verify the information you've given us..."

"Verify?"

"Yes, find out if what you're saying is true..."

I walked out of the welfare office both angry and feeling low. There was a three month waiting period. The phone was cut off. Things were rough.

Kevin and I got up the next morning. I got dressed and went to the liquor store. Maybe I can meet somebody new. If it happens today, it won't be too soon. I wasn't going to be nobody's ho. But I had to do what I had to do, in order to make that dough.

I was walking, pushing my baby's stroller, scheming on figures when I spotted her, Bernice walking solo. I approached her. It was close to lunch and she offered me a meal. She wanted to know what I was doing out here. At first I tried to lie but she could see straight through them. Finally, I confessed.

"I got caught up. I had a baby for this no-good sonnofabitch. He hasn't even tried to spend any money on us," I said pointing to Kevin asleep in his stroller.

"Damn, but shit do happens..."

"Please, tell me about it..."

"Your son is so cute," Bernice said and that made me smile.

"I'm gonna raise him the best I can."

"That was my intentions with my daughter, before that no good uncle of yours messed up her whole life."

I thought about what Bernice had said and realized that she was really angry. She let her tears out.

We ate and for my child's sake I had to keep it moving. Bernice talked about her daughter going for therapy and staying three days at a time because she was experiencing nightmares.

"It's been real, but I gotta go..."

"Samone, I hope you don't mind. I'll take care of lunch and here, take this."

She handed me fifty dollars. I didn't want to take it. I felt super low, this was way beneath me, but it was survival. She wasn't as bad a person as daddy and Uncle Black had made her out to be. I promised to see her again and we hugged as I left.

On the way home all I thought of was what could I do to help her in return.

# 31 | SUGAR MAMA

It was a nice spring day and me and my son was out. I was so happy that Carefree's mother had bought Kevin a new and better stroller. I kept thinking Kevin needed a real father, not the fake-ass one he had. It was about time I found him one. We reached Girard Street liquor store. I spotted someone I knew. He saw my son and immediately he had to make a move in his Blazer. The taxi driver was a girl's best friend and it was a whole lot better than walking.

I stopped in the mall window shopping. It felt good to be alive, I thought leaving out of a store, and some guy held the door for me. He watched me pushing the stroller down the street.

Another dude said: "What's up sugar mama?"

I smiled, gave him a small glance and waved like I was royalty.

"Can I go with you?" he asked.

I motioned with my finger and he did just what I asked. I loved when boys do exactly what I asked. I played along.

"What's you name sugar mama?"

"I like sugar mama, but it is Samone. And yours?"

"Raynard, they call me Ray."

Ray had a nugget bracelet, nugget ring, and one long Gucci link chain with a Jesus medallion, sporting diamonds on the crown. My bottom lips twitched. I smelled money.

"Ray, huh...?"

"Yeah sugar mama, meet me on Fairmont. I'm going to take you and your lil' shortie here to get something to eat and buy him some pampers and some Enfamil. It's five thirty I'll meet you at six. Better yet sugar mama, meet me at the gas station. I'm going to get a bottle of Dom and you can go with me." He said sizing me up.

Ray pulled up in an Audi. He threw the stroller in the trunk and off we went. We made a pit stop at Florida Avenue Grill. He got out, hopped in some other dude's car. Ray started pulling bundles of money out of his pockets. My eyes went wide. Lord he has to be my friend! Ray went to the trunk and came back with the bottle of Dom. He poured me a cup and off we went. Kevin asleep in one arm and sipping, feeling right nice. Our next stop was Safeway. Ray disappeared inside. Minutes later he reappeared with pampers and Enfamil.

"How did you know?" I asked.

"Sugar Mama I've been watching you for a minute." I know you deal with the dude. You stay cussing him out. I heard him say earlier that you're pissed off that the phone is off and rent ain't right."

"Damn you know a lot, huh?"

"Mama, you live on Ontario Road right."

"Oh, you definitely did your homework."

"I'm going to take care of all that. I'll give you all that tomorrow all right."

"Thanks, Ray," I said batting my eyelids hard.

"You're welcome sugar mama. Anything you want I'm going to make it happen."

Ray looked good in his red Fila velour sweat suit and matching Applejack Kangol.

"I'm going to give you my pager number and this code. Give me your home number, and all that will be out of the way. Just go to the phone booth in the morning and page me with your code. Don't call me when your baby-daddy's there."

"Alright," I replied with a broad smile.

He pulled up in front of Hogates. The rum buns were delicious. I ordered a lobster platter and Ray ordered the same thing. After we ate, he dropped me off on Lanier. I was on cloud nine.

I fed Kevin bathed him and the phone rang. I looked dumbfounded.

"Hello, you paid the bill? Yeah alright, I see you later." Carefree was real stupid. That was his way of hanging out. Phone should have never been off in the first place. I hit up Ray.

"I guess he paid that, huh?" Ray asked when he came on the phone.

"Yeah..."

"Good man. I'm a little busy. I'm going to call you later."

That was it. Carefree had played himself for the last time. The fool came home with a passion mark on his genitals. I sent that nigga on his way for real. His ass was a trip. He knew I never sucked his dick. He was always talking about he wanted to eat some fish. At first, I thought the fool wanted me to fry him some fish. That night, he came home ready with Moet. Kevin was with his grandmother.

Carefree pulled out a joint. Turned on the blue light on and said: "Let me show you the fish I want. Relax, baby," he said as he took my clothes off.

He sucked my nipples slowly then hard. He squeezed both so tight, while licking my stomach. Then he slid his tongue between my legs and I felt his warm tongue sucking on my clitoris. My eyes rolled in the back of my head, feeling a pleasure I never felt before. He started sucking it as if it was a straw. Next thing I knew he stuck two fingers in my ass and pussy simultaneously.

I squirmed as he began moving his digits in and out. My mind felt like it was about to explode. I grabbed his head and raked his back with my nails. I didn't know what else to do or what to expect. The liquor and weed had me going and suddenly my actions became so wild. I felt like I was going to lose my mind and started screaming going crazy, yelling.

"Stop, no don't stop...ah gosh yes Lord. Help me, give it to me. Oh, ah yeah..."

No matter how loud I screamed, Carefree wouldn't stop. It was like he wanted the world to know that I was getting my fish eaten. I had never had an orgasm like that before.

I was going to miss all that, but this broke-ass nigga had me caught up for a minute and when I went to return the favor I saw the passion mark. That was the last straw. It more than broke my back.

"I can do what I want. I pays all the fucking bills up in here." He screamed at me.

"Not no fucking more you sonnofabitch! You don't do a fucking thing. Niggas like you will have a bitch on pins and needles. Get out of here with all your bullshit and take them shirts you bought for me. You might need them more than me. Leave my keys you sorry ass sonnofabitch!"

"Samone," he said when the reality of losing me had set in.

"Whatcha want nigga?"

"Can I use your phone?"

"Go use the bitch's phone that put that red sore on your dick. Now get the fuck out!"

Carefree had fucked up my night. Now I really needed Ray to come over. He invited me instead. I caught a cab over to Ray house. I reached upstairs and saw money piled up five stacks high. Ray was a show-off but he wasn't stingy. His sex was good. I mean he punished me. I must admit, it was a most pleasurable hurting.

I saw female underwears while showering but said nothing. I needed a few of those twenties. Kevin needs pampers. Ray started coming over but not as much as I would have liked him to. He started playing 'not-answer-the-pager' game for days at a time. His excuse; he was out of town.

This went on for awhile until Marina told me that she had seen him at the Anita Baker show with another girl. When I confronted him, he cried it was a lie. I was sick of men and their lame excuses. I did not speak to him for nearly two weeks.

One night Ray popped up with some Dom and we rocked like we did when we had first met.

That night, Carefree must have called three times trying to make-up. My phone rang all night long.

Even though Carefree was my son's father, Ray would hit me off and always left me dough. That gave him the advantage to my pussy. Carefree would want to just show up for visits and always trying to hit it for free. I wasn't having it. I had no babysitter and had to make hay while my sun shined. When things were good, Ray had access to my ass. I knew Ray wasn't all good either.

The investigators finally came out and questioned my landlord. Thank God my bills were finally paid and I was able to go out and shop for food. I made sure that it was plentiful.

# 32 | KEVIN'S FIRST BIRTHDAY

The phone was ringing off the hook. Every few minutes it would be ring, ring, ring, I rushed to get it.

"Hello...Ray what's up?"

"What's up baby?"

"Nothing much, just getting ready for your stepson to turn one in a couple of days."

"Yeah, that's right, that lil man been here for twelve months now. Why don't you come by the club and pick some money up for him so he can enjoy his first year. I know that sorry-ass Carefree ain't gonna do nothing for him. I heard your daddy wanted to kill him? Can't see how a man doesn't take care of his responsibilities."

I could hear the anger in his voice and quickly changed the subject.

"I'm planning to take Kevin to Virginia for his birthday."

"I'll give you an extra hundred for the round trip ticket."

When Kevin turned one, I bought a sheet cake with his face on it. Enough sea food and chicken was prepared for everyone. There were people who wondered where the money came from. But they just eat, and sang happy birthday to my baby. He looked good in his white suit.

Later that night, Carefree called to find out if he could come by. I knew Ray was coming over so I declined and told him to come by tomorrow evening.

"Your son is sleeping anyway. Why didn't you come by earlier? Come tomorrow. Goodnight." I hung up.

The door bell rang and Ray came in. He started to eat some cake then gave me the gifts and money. He offered to take me and Kevin on a shopping spree. Ray ate and left. Kevin was asleep and I felt lonely. I drank some wine and just as I was about to smoke a joint, there was a knock on the door.

"Who...?" I asked thinking that Ray had returned for something he had left. "Ray, is that you?"

The voice surprised me.

"Open the door it ain't Ray. Open the door, now."

Carefree entered with toys in his hand. I stared dumbfounded at him. "Ain't you gonna invite me to eat like you did your man. Go ahead light that joint."

"I don't want to smoke anymore," I said.

"Yeah, sure..."

He grabbed the joint and lit it. He swallowed smoke as he looked around the place.

"Had you a good party, huh?"

"Yeah, but I'm really tired. I appreciate the gift and all that but you gotta go."

"You kicking me out without letting me see my son."

"All right, go take a look at him, he's in the bedroom."

"Walk with me," he said grabbing my arm.

"I don't have time..."

"Yes, you do."

I walked with him to the baby's crib. We stood watching our son sleep. Whatever was on Carefree's mind, I was ready for him to go. He tried to kiss me but I slipped out of his grip.

"You not gonna give me a good-night kiss?" he asked.

"See, you're acting up. You got to go for real, for real, Carefree. I don't have time. I'm tired."

"You wouldn't be tired if it was Ray." He said and grabbed me harder.

I resisted. He pushed me and I ran to the kitchen and grabbed the butcher knife. Carefree met me and slapped the shit out of me. I fell on the floor and he was on me, beating me like I was a man. He ripped my clothes off and kneed me in my stomach. Then he pried my legs open and unzipped his pants. I managed to wrest my legs free and kicked him in the groin. He punched me in the face then tried to push his dick in me. It wasn't going down like that tonight.

"Carefree, you gonna get some cold ass pussy, because you're gonna have to kill me before I let you between my legs." I yelled struggling.

I fought and scratched and clawed. I didn't care. This

man was not going to rape me without a fight.

The baby was screaming and my fighting seemed to excite Carefree. He tried harder and harder, slapping me, ripping my clothes to shreds. He realized he was going to have to kill me in order to get some pussy. Finally Carefree let me up. I chased him out of my apartment with the butcher knife.

I stared at my maimed reflection in the bathroom. This was crazy. He must think he was in a boxing match. I was severely beaten over what was between my legs. I washed my face, went into the room and hugged my baby.

"Don't you ever do this to any woman, Kevin," I whispered hushing my baby.

I stayed away from school and ignored all phone calls. For about a week I was inside, not because I was scared but because I needed time for the bruises to heal.

Ray didn't call and I didn't care. This time I was through with men. I wanted nothing to do with any of them.

One day I went downstairs for fresh air. It had been nearly two weeks that I had stayed cooped inside the apartment. The first person I ran in to was Bernice.

"Hey Samone, how...Oh my God what the hell happened? You look like you were in a boxing match."

"It was a car accident," I lied.

"I hope you're gonna have big insurance settlement." She said but it was plain she didn't believe a word I had said. "Oh boy, your son is growing..."

"That's not really what happened," I said.

I explained how I really sustained the bruises.

"Are you gonna keep taking the abuse, Samone? You've got his child and if he can disrespect you once and you do nothing about it, then he'll keep doing it. You've got to do something."

"But what can I do?"

"You can file charges and get that motherfucker locked up. Why don't you come with me and see that DA I was telling you about."

"But...you mean go against my...?"

"Yes you could put your uncle behind bars and all the men like Carefree, who think they can stick their dicks wherever... whenever...in whoever..."

I thought about it, sighed and invited Bernice upstairs. She explained and I listened intently. Before I knew it, she was calling the DA and triumphantly announcing my allegiance to whatever the plan was.

"They'll see you tomorrow..." She said when she got off the phone. "Now you can tell them everything Samone..."

I stared at my baby boy sleeping peacefully. Going to the DA and telling everything will be the end of the relationship between me my entire family. I could wound up sitting on the witness stand, facing my uncle, daddy and male cousins as defendants.

I sat contemplating whether or not I was ready to take sides against my family like that. Would the backlash of their alienation be worth it?

My heartbeat came loud and fast as I looked at my son. He was innocently asleep. My thoughts stirred with his every move. There was no other way to think. The bruises were still fresh, I had to act now. I didn't need another damn minute to think about my decision. I just have to deal with the consequences and repercussions that would surely come.

# The End

## IMPORTANT STATS

About 2 out of 1000 children in the United States were confirmed by child protective service agencies as having experienced sexual assault in 2003 (DHHS 2005). See child maltreatment fact sheet for more information.

- Among high school youth nationwide:
- About 9% of students reported that they had been forced to have sexual intercourse.
- Female students are more likely than male students to report sexual assault (11.9% vs. 6.1%).
- Overall, 12.3% of Black students, 10.4% of Hispanic students, and 7.3% of White students reported that they had been forced to have sexual intercourse (CDC 2004).
- Among college students nationwide, between 20% and 25% of women reported experiencing completed or attempted rape (Fisher, Cullen, and Turner 2000).
- Among adults nationwide:
- More than 300,000 women (0.3%) and over 90,000 men (0.1%) reported being raped in the previous 12 months.
- One in six women (17%) and one in thirty-three men (3%) reported experiencing an attempted or completed rape at some time in their lives.

Abuse, and Incest National Network (RAINN) operates the National Sexual Assault Hotline at 1-800-656-HOPE.

# [ LITERALLY DOPE ]

**GHETTO GIRLS (SPECIAL EDITION)**
ANTHONY WHYTE

**GHETTO GIRLS TOO**
ANTHONY WHYTE

**GHETTO GIRLS 3: SOO HOOD**
ANTHONY WHYTE

**THE BLUE CIRCLE**
KEISHA SEIGNIOUS

**BOOTY CALL *69**
ERICK S GRAY

**IF IT AIN'T ONE THING IT'S ANOTHER**
SHARRON DOYLE

**IT CAN HAPPEN IN A MINUTE**
S.M. JOHNSON

Llanto de la mujer

WOMAN'S *cry*

A NOVEL BY
VANESSA MARTIR

**Woman's Cry** is a Latina look on Hip Hop fiction. It is a Span-glish novella with unexpected twists and turns that will keep the reader enthralled in this urban drama.

Renee Maldonado is a senior at Columbia University and is busy living two opposite lives. Her love for a drug dealer takes her down a dangerous path of trying to hold on to something that's out of her control. She has to turn her life around and realizes that every action brings an unexpected reaction. Renee sees the perilous nature of her decisions and realizes she could gain the world at the cost of losing her soul.

A NOVEL BY
# VENESSA MARTIR

"Llanto De La Mujer is a riveting tale, cleverly concocted by first time author, Vanessa Martir. Woman's Cry is sure to be a winner."

A NOVEL BY

# JAMES HENDRICKS

THE BLUE CIRCLE

KEISHA SEIGNIOUS

The Blue Circle is a gripping fast paced drama jumping off at the beginning of the Hip Hop era. The explosion of the culture is a visual backdrop. Up in the Bronx where the people are fresh, The Blue Circle was the favorite hangout for b-boys and girls. As the culture grows so does the bond between four friends. Dawn, Keya, Forster, and Cash met at The Blue Circle. Dawn juggles real love with her parents' self centered dreams. Keya is from a decent family, but her life transforms as she struggles with being a single teen parent. Forster and Cash are diehard friends, not even dough could separate them. Starting young in the street game, their pockets grew along with their attitudes. Envy and jealousy threaten these friendships until tragedy occurs. Forster has known Dawn since their teenage days and certainly never considered her a potential wife...until an unexpected heated kiss that brought hope and changes for all. Will they make it down the altar? Or must Forster Pay with his life for Cash's beef?

The Blue Circle is the hot debut novel from a talented writer, Keisha Seignious. Based on a real NYC story, this exciting page-turner examines the scathing aspects of friendship, family interactions and true love.

A NOVEL BY
KEISHA SEGNIOUS

"The Blue Circle is an evocative and shockingly delightful novel that captures you from the very first page!"
— Crystal Lacey Winslow (author of The Criss Cross and Life, Love & Loneliness)

A NOVEL BY
SHARRON DOYLE

it ain't one thing it's another

A richly textured story of deceit; **If It Ain't One Thing It's Another,** is the most riveting tale of the decade. Every once in a while an author comes along with dazzling talents. In her debut novel, **It Ain't One Thing It's Another,** Sharron Doyle broke us off with this sensational tale of vengeance, thirst and hunger.

Streetwise, Petie is grinding on the road to infamy. His throne is toppled and his rule is coming to an end. He will not be kingpin, but he's bent on taking his family, his mistress, Share', best friend and fellow hustler, Ladell, through their most traumatic experiences. On lockdown, Petie is no snitch and does not cooperate with the justice department. After being released Petie's twisted method of exacting revenge on his enemies will shock and open the eyes of every reader. He comes armed to the nines ready to get rid of those who snitched or betrayed him. Only Share' stands in his way. His enemies soon find out that: **If Ain't One Thing It's Another** is revenge at all cost. Beef never dies, it multiplies.

# A NOVEL BY
# SHARRON DOYLE

"A fast paced hood chiller! This story is destined to be the talk of the town. The story grabs you and just does not let go."

-Anthony Whyte (Bestselling author of Ghetto Girls Series)